THE LABYRINTH

An alumnus of Presidency College, Calcutta, **Udayan Majumdar** has, in the past, worked as a journalist, and is currently the editor of a credit rating company. His short stories have been published in *The Statesman*. This is his debut novel.

THE ABSOLUTE

The Labyrinth

Udayan Majumdar

RUPA

Published by
Rupa Publications India Pvt. Ltd 2013
7/16, Ansari Road, Daryaganj
New Delhi 110002

Sales Centres:
Allahabad Bengaluru Chennai
Hyderabad Jaipur Kathmandu
Kolkata Mumbai

ISBN: 978-81-291-2416-6

10 9 8 7 6 5 4 3 2 1

The moral right of the author has been asserted.

Typeset by Saanavi Graphics, Noida

Printed at Parksons Graphics Pvt Ltd., Taloja

To the memory of my father
Asish Kumar Majumdar

The Labyrinth

The labyrinth begins, in the three dimensions of Euclid, deep inside a forest in the eastern Indian state oddly named West Bengal. On the dimension of time, it goes back about two decades and a half from now, the unseen jailer's clock starting to tick as I first meet the elderly gentleman, Shri Dwarakanath Chatterjee, on a ribbon-like strip of red murram amidst the verdant bloom of his ancient estate. It is from here in space and time that the winding desire path meanders out of the realm of the sal, mahogany, neem and mehul into varied panoramas, distant landscapes to complete its confounding convolutions.

Often, at the halfway halt between resignation and fear, the mind invokes on the dark, suede side of my eyelids the tortuous course of the labyrinth, and I sometimes fancy placing at the approach of each of the deluding turns, appropriate glow-in-the-dark signboards with such luminescent warnings as: the call of destiny; the awakening; the black box; forsaken; the garden of Eden...

But I wander.

Let me begin at the beginning—in innocence and wonder.

The Call of Destiny

Circa 1985. Summer holidays. I was rotting in my college hostel, deserted by most boarder friends and foes, who for their part were visiting their own friends and foes, some within their respective families, others without. Keeping me company at the Government Eden Hindu Hostel, a century-old red-brick structure that was once unwittingly home to a future president (and his brother), were the two durwans of the hostel, Hoshiyar Singh and Jung Bahadur Thapa, from my native town of Ranchi and Darjeeling, respectively. And there was of course the hapless bookworm, the third-year zoology student, Patra, initially rechristened Kelo Patra in jest ('kelo' meaning 'darkie' and 'goof' as well) and finally Cleopatra!

I would usually spend the mornings with Thapada watching him draw plants and insects for the botany and zoology students who had left their lab notebooks with him, and admiring the dexterity with which he diced vegetables at the shrill command of his martinet wife.

The evenings however were set aside for the usually reclusive Hoshiyarji. After he'd had his grass and his eyes were bloodshot, the portly gatekeeper would come over to my room to invite me to the small patch of green that the L-shaped Hindu Hostel had within its compound. And once we had settled down, facing each other on his sagging charpoy, he would invariably travel back to his days as a lorry driver at a Ranchi-based timber company in an era long past, evoking with his dramatic bass the land of waterfalls, lakes and wind-swayed paddy fields in a bizarre mix of Bhojpuri and Hindi. A minute or two into the narration, he would take two beedis and a matchbox out of the folds of his lungi and ask me to light both; one for him, the other for me. And by the time he had taken a few drags, he would be at the wheel of Raja Begum once again, either driving the nine-tonne lorry out of or into Ranchi, the city where I had my schooling and where my parents still lived. Besides Hoshiyarji's numerous adventures with his king/queen of lorries, what held my fascination was an uncanny trait in him: often, in the midst of some hair-raising narrative, he would come out with something completely irrelevant, only to be vindicated later.

That evening, I had been transported to a winding dirt road in the Hazaribagh forest which Raja Begum was then negotiating with a full load of timber on his/her cavernous back, when Hoshiyarji braked suddenly and asked, 'But where would the road be taking you, babu?' Surprised, I said I had no plans of going anywhere soon. He looked away, nodded to himself and almost sighed, 'But it would be taking you far, very far babu, and also bringing you back some day...'

Moments later, the hostel telephone let out its piercing ring and I had to go for it, knowing Hoshiyarji's dialect post-grass would be incomprehensible to any caller and it would take Cleopatra ages to wiggle out of his textbook.

The excited voice of Mrinalini—Mrinalini Mukherjee, my classmate at Presidency College—at the other end stumped me.

'I'm going to my grandpa's by the six o'clock Ispat Express tomorrow morning,' she chirped, 'for about a fortnight. Want to come along? Say yes Sudipto, please...'

'Sure, of course!' I exclaimed and after a brief chat returned bewildered to Hoshiyarji.

'So where would you be going babu?' Hoshiyarji asked and when I told him it was to a forest in Jhargram, his forehead creased in a frown. 'Why, what's wrong?' I poked him, but the inscrutable gatekeeper would not elaborate. It was only after some pestering that he said he too had been in love with the jungle once, but the jungle was a jealous lover and would suffer no other paramour. And with that he fell silent again, nodding occasionally to himself. Hoshiyarji, I thought, was yet to come to terms with the absence of a woman in his life.

~

Jhargram had long fascinated me although I had not visited the place ever. The South Eastern Railway's Howrah-Hatia Express that I routinely took to travel home to Ranchi did have a scheduled halt at Jhargram, but I had never so much as set foot on the small railway station encircled by ancient sal, mahogany and neem jutting out of the red earth as if to complete a canvas of scarlet, blue and brilliant green.

Actually, the invitation to visit Jhargram had not come out of the blue.

My interest in the sleepy forest town in the Midnapore district of West Bengal, not far from the borders of Bihar, had been kindled by Mrinalini. It had so happened that in one of those homesick moments, I had confided in her my longing for the land of my childhood. I had told her how, at the most inopportune of times, something nameless would tug at my heart; how the scent of raindrops on the parched earth would bring back memories in all their vibrant colours; how in lonely moments the inky blue sky with its million stars hanging over our house would beckon me.

She could make sense of it all, she said, because of what Jhargram had given her.

An 'émigré' from the small town of Ranchi—a part of undivided Bihar then—my heart still belonged to the small room in which I had grown up from an innocent infant to a bumbling matriculate. True, I had always yearned to be in the bustling city of Calcutta with its tramcars and double-decker buses, but once in the metropolis, I soon realized Ranchi would hold my heartstrings forever. It was not seldom that I would be carried away to my haunts in my hometown, to be lost among trees, in the wilderness, in the stretching green fields peering from behind the heaving sheer curtains in my little room. Sometimes, I would find my wraith lying still on the small lawn of our house, staring at the autumn sky with its tufts of wind-rushed clouds floating by. Or I would be on all fours in the overgrown tetragon (once a kitchen garden) at the back, watching tiny creatures carry on diligently with the business of living. At times I would laugh out loud remembering the wild excitement of having caught tadpoles—convinced they were fish—from the inundated paddy fields, having braved a torrential downpour, ankle-deep slush and my mother's warnings.

All this I had shared with Mrinalini, and she had said we were perhaps soul mates for she would go through something similar for days together every time she returned from Jhargram, where her grandfather lived with a handful of servants in a sprawling estate deep inside a sal forest.

From then on, soaking in numerous stories of Jhargram during those stolen moments with Mrinalini at Pramodda's, the Presidency College hangout, I too fell in love with the place.

And gradually this fondness for an Arden not discovered grew into a kind of longing. I had often urged Mrinalini to take me to her grandpa's, but something or the other had always stood in the way of an invitation. That is, till the piercing ring of the hostel telephone.

The next morning we met under the 'boro ghari'—big clock, Howrah station's most familiar fixture—as planned, and about three hours later found ourselves standing on the railway platform at Jhargram, my head reeling with the anticipation of future thrills. We got into a bus along with a crowd of mostly tribal men, chirpy women with large baskets of clucking hens, and a couple of nervous goats. Eventually, the wheezing and clanking vehicle dropped us under a huge tree with a lime-washed trunk in the middle of nowhere; there was no sign of anything even remotely resembling the bungalow I had heard so much about. I turned to Mrinalini only to find her looking at me with a twinkle in her eyes.

'Westward Ho!' she broke into a smile, 'We'll have to walk the rest of it.'

But I stood rooted to the spot, the fairy queen's empire of scarlet and emerald weaving its magic in whorls of radiance around me even as my eyes followed her raised hand pointing at the dirt track weaving its way through ancient trees and an old-world village that lay ahead.

'We'll go beyond that tiny village, take a short cut through the forest and cross a canal to get to the estate,' the queen proclaimed.

A heavy fragrance hung in the air, and I closed my eyes drawing it in with a deep breath. 'That's mehul,' the voice tinkled from somewhere very close, sending me into a swoon. 'Mahua blossoms have this intoxicating fragrance. See...'

I looked at her and then following her eyes, saw the ivory

flowers scattered at our feet. We were standing under a large mahua tree.

'The villagers here brew these for a heady drink. Want to try some?'

'Who would need a drink in such a place!' I said. The fairy queen squeezed my hand and kept holding it.

We began our trek, following the red dirt track that ran through the middle of the village like the vermillion-marked parting of a bride's hair, until we came to a point where another track looping in from the forest ahead joined the one we were on to form an untutored Y. Now, we had either to take the left arm or the one right. The queen appeared confused. She said she had always come to Jhargram by car, by the road that led to the estate from the Bombay Highway, and chewed her lip fretfully even as I looked around, charmed.

Presently, a clearly sozzled villager with a crooked stick tottered out of the forest and appeared quite taken aback to find us, city people, at such an unlikely place. He stood still for long, staring at Mrinalini and mumbling something about her 'pentool' (trousers), before asking us in a curious mix of Santhali and Bangla where we intended to go. I told him we were trying to get to Shri Dwarakanath Chatterjee's estate at which he steadied himself and pointed in the direction of the winding trail:

'Hooyi Chatterjeebabur bagan.'

I would have thanked him but his mumbling about Mrinalini's trousers had got on my nerves. And the lady in question only added to my outrage with her giggle, saying she would gift me a fainting couch on my next birthday. The result was that the forest came and went and so did the promised canal, even as all I did was to follow in Mrinalini's footsteps, agitated and muttering under my breath all the way up to her grandpa's estate.

The Awakening

'Chatterjeebabur Bagan' was quite a large one, fenced by a shaggy hedge laden with white sickly-sweet blossoms. So large was it that the bungalow appeared small from the rickety gate made out of a few dozen intricately arranged bamboo splints. We pushed open the handicraft and as it creaked wide to let us in, there he was, Shri Dwarakanath Chatterjee, Mrinalini's grandpa, a tallish gentleman with a shock of silky white hair, round glasses and a benevolent smile, walking down the red murram path actually to welcome us.

'Since morning I've had this hunch there would be visitors today. I've been here walking up and down for the past half an hour,' he said as he smothered his granddaughter in an embrace. Then turning towards me, he asked, 'Where is it that I have seen you earlier, Baba?' And before I could say I had no idea, he took my hand in his. 'You're welcome, most welcome,' he said, looking at me affectionately.

I touched his feet and with that my life had taken a new turn.

~

The fortnight I spent at Jhargram is a tale good enough to last a lifetime. But how should I begin? I wish I had the flair of Hoshiyarji, or even Thapada for that matter.

My first few minutes at the sprawling estate of Chatterjeebabu, whom I shall henceforth call Dadu, were a kind of awakening: awakening to the world of stately trees; to the world of shifting shadows, evocative fragrances and lingering silences, punctuated by birdsongs.

'Dadu's bungalow is at least as ancient as your Hindu Hostel, if not more,' Mrinalini said, breaking my trance, and snatching away my haversack, put it down beside her faux crocodile-leather bag in a corner of the outsized sitting room that we had just entered. 'Come Sudipto, let me show you around,' she gushed and I gladly followed.

I was shown into three large bedrooms, each with a double bed, a table, a wardrobe with an oval mirror and a few chairs.

'Everything here is made of mahogany and sal—and all that comes from our garden,' she declared, oozing pride.

'You make mirrors too?' I ventured, and got a sharp pinch for an answer.

In the bedroom on the west, which Mrinalini said was hers, there was a huge book rack occupying two adjacent walls from the floor to the false ceiling, stacked with countless books, several bound in burgundy morocco leather. The bedrooms apart, there was a fairly large washroom tucked away in one corner of the bungalow—an English toilet, complete with a basin counter but surprisingly, no taps.

'There's no running water here,' Mrinalini had anticipated my question. 'The old world still lingers in Jhargram. Pails of freshly drawn water service the household. And guess what, in winter we leave the filled buckets outside for the sun to warm! Come, I'll show you our water supply.'

I was led outside to a large well, complete with a pulley, a giant iron pail shaped like the conical cap of a ballistic missile, and a coiled coir rope, basking in the sun.

'What do you know of echoes?' Mrinalini asked, an eyebrow raised, and leaning into the well in a twinkling, let out a sudden whoop that made me jump. The well called back.

'Your turn now,' she laughed even as I hesitated for a moment before letting slip the only word swirling in my head then: 'Mrinaaaalini!'

Nothing happened. The call was too feeble to stir up the echoes.

'Hey, what happened to your voice? Why don't you lean in? You won't fall baba... Yeah, that's it...now shout...no long words, just a syllable or two... Come on...'

The complexity of the command, especially the limit of two syllables, made me somewhat nervous and bending over the circular wall, I foolishly yelled 'Lini'. The echoes understood my plight. 'Nee...nee...' they obliged, even as Mrinalini gaped at me, her mouth open, caught between cheering and chiding.

'"Nee" in German is "never" in English if I remember right,' Dadu appeared from behind a lofty sal clutching a bunch of yard long beans and some green chillies. 'Breakfast will soon be served,' he smiled, holding up his harvest as he walked away towards the cluster of guava trees that appeared to screen a few brick-and-mud huts lying scattered behind the bungalow.

'What are those?' I asked my guide.

'Ruins of Mohenjo Daro, the Mound of the Dead,' she whispered, rolling her eyes as she lugged me towards them. There were five huts: a kitchen, a dining hall, a prayer room, the servants' quarters, and the most unusual bathroom I have ever seen—one without a ceiling! Apparently, the job of protecting the modesty of bathers from unlikely aerial voyeurs had been delegated to a large neem tree that stood guard on the immediate left of the decapitated structure, spreading its massive branches over its walls. A little distance from this remarkable bath house were

a few mahua trees, one of them particularly large with a small
cemented area around it and what looked like a seat at its base.

The main entrance to the bungalow opened to a large
cemented courtyard, where four charpoys, in much the same
condition as Hoshiyarji's way back at Hindu Hostel, had been
placed in no particular pattern. And on one side were a few bushels
of raw cashew nuts, probably the last of the season, spread out
to dry in the sun. To the right, as Mrinalini pointed out, was a
bed of tulsi watched over by a large peepul, and beyond that
a kitchen garden, its perimeter marked by a row of plantains.

'That's our supply of dinner plates,' Mrinalini exclaimed,
pointing to the banana leaves, and appeared completely deflated
when I said we too had our meals on banana leaves at Ranchi
when our major-domo failed to show up for days at a stretch.

We now crossed over to the left of the courtyard, I still
relishing the triumph over leaf plates, when without any warning
Mrinalini let loose a barrage of complicated never-heard-of
names, pointing to trees of various shapes and sizes to my utter
bewilderment. I staggered under the onslaught, and it is only
when she came to the common labels of the mango, guava and
jackfruit that I breathed easy, the familiar tags of the sal and
mahogany finally getting me home.

'Where did you pick up so much from?' I asked, 'considering
you have grown up in the city?'

She squeezed my hand and laughed, 'I was born wild, you see!'

The tour over, we returned to the courtyard to have our
delayed breakfast of luchi and 'bagan chochchodi', a dish that
Dadu said his Man Friday, Shibu, would prepare with the day's
pick of vegetables from the kitchen garden. Shibuda, I noted, was
a middle-aged Santhal, with jet black hair, taut and polished skin,
sparkling white teeth with two prominent canines sticking out

from beneath a bushy moustache, and a complexion that could compete with my friend Cleopatra's. For some reason he would call me 'jamata', literally son-in-law, which was rather awkward, but Dadu, instead of correcting him, merely smiled.

Breakfast was followed by a round of chess between two Geminis—Dadu and I—who not only had a common birthday, but also a similar style of manoeuvring chessmen on the sixty-four squares. The tussle went on for over an hour, much to Mrinalini's exasperation, and eventually youth managed to score over experience.

'Here cometh the sole cause of my inglorious defeat,' Dadu declared as he looked in the direction of the bamboo gate. Pointing at the man walking slowly towards us, he explained, smiling all the while, 'Mothur is such a miserable opponent that I've forgotten how to defend.'

I stood up as the gentleman with salt-and-pepper hair, a thick drooping moustache of the same chromatic combination, skin a shade lighter than Shibuda's, and a slight limp came up to our charpoy. After Dadu had introduced me to him, he shook my hand vigorously, took a long look at the chessboard, and with a gleam in his eyes asked who had won the game. When Dadu said it was not him, Mothurbabu let out a war cry and did a small jig, with the result that the can of milk he was carrying spilt much of its contents even as Dadu roared with laughter and I looked on embarrassed.

Mothurbabu, like Hoshiyarji, proved a natural storyteller. Once Dadu went indoors to have a chat with his granddaughter, Mothurbabu settled down to apply himself to the task of explaining his 'case' to me. He was a caretaker at the estate next to Dadu's. He lived there with his wife, two teenage sons, and five milch cows, which being 'spotlessly black' produced the best milk in the entire Midnapore district, what to talk of Jhargram. The landlord never visited the estate and had stopped sending him his salary since several years back, but that did not bother Mothurbabu. The estate that he looked after and now almost owned had a large eucalyptus plantation, and these days there was never a dearth of pharmaceutical companies seeking to take the plantation on lease. His only worry, he said, were elephants.

'Elephants? Oh I would love to see one here!' I exclaimed.

'You would not, if you saw my wife,' Mothurbabu said, putting on a glum face.

I burst out laughing at the imagined sight of a woolly mammoth masquerading as Mothurbabu's demure consort.

'What is there to laugh?' Mothurbabu appeared quite offended, correctly guessing the vision I had just conjured. 'My wife is not like an elephant. In fact, she was quite pretty once. And fair too.'

I said I was sorry, and Mothurbabu, good natured that he was, accepted my apology readily. Just a few months back, he said, a herd of elephants had descended on the place and ravaged it. It was almost an annual ritual. They would eat up all the banana plants and slender bamboo stems and generally break and plunder whatever they did not find to their liking.

'When they walk, they're as silent as cats,' Mothurbabu whispered. 'Pity, she had to learn it the hard way.'

I was intrigued, but Mothurbabu would not elaborate. He said there was a cartload of odd jobs awaiting his return and he had better hurry. It was only when Shibuda appeared with his kettle of tea and two earthen tumblers that Mothurbabu agreed to defer his departure and establish the link between rogue elephants and his fair wife.

The 'time would be about 5 a.m. in the morning' when Mothurbabu's wife had got up to gather flowers for the morning prayers. But the moment she stepped out of the house she found this huge rogue of a tusker right in her way, staring at her. Mothurbabu's wife let out a scream, which her husband, still in bed and his snoring interrupted, read as religious ecstasy; he did find the subsequent noises somewhat intriguing, he admitted, but they were not serious enough for immediate investigation, he presumed.

It was only about half an hour or so later when Mothurbabu left his bed and wobbled out into his estate looking for his herbal toothbrush—slender neem twigs—that he discovered the havoc the elephants had created. He called out for his wife repeatedly and with increasing alarm but there was no response. He panicked. Mothurbabu's sons woke up in the commotion caused by their trumpeting father, remained perplexed for some time and finally shot out 'like bullets from a double-barrel gun' to look for their missing mother. A quarter of an hour's search later, Mothurbabu's wife was discovered lying unconscious in the plundered bamboo grove with several of her bones broken and a gash on her forehead. The beast had picked her up and flung her, but thankfully refrained from trampling her, which elephants often do.

The 'medicinal treatment' had been long and expensive, involving several visits to the Calcutta Medical College, and had drained Mothurbabu of all his savings.

'Even now my wife can't squat,' Mothurbabu rued as he got up to leave. He yelled goodbye to Dadu, congratulated me on my chess game, and limped away towards the bamboo gate, leaving me to wonder what tragedy lay behind his own unusual gait.

Shibuda came in to take the kettle away and told me lunch would be ready soon, which meant I would have to take my bath immediately. To my consternation I learnt it was the outdoor bathroom I would have to use. At Hindu Hostel I was used to bathing in the open veranda, where we had attached one end of a garden pipe to the basin tap and at the other fixed a shower head, but the prospect of taking a bath in a roofless bathroom with civilized gentry around was awkward. The actual act was however not as public or uncomfortable as I had feared and the cool water of the well quite refreshing.

We had lunch in the dining hall, with Shibuda's smiling wife Phulmoni and two of their sons, both well-built and pleasantly polite, serving the food and pouring water into our earthen tumblers. The dining hall had a large mahogany table with eight chairs, besides an enormous earthen pitcher of drinking water resting on a red cloth turban in a corner. Guarding the pitcher, it seemed to me, was a large golden-yellow frog with beady eyes and a demeanour that was somewhat severe as it stared at me. The thick brown rice, daal, okra fry, mixed vegetables and egg curry served one after the other on our leaf plates however took my attention away from the frog, and I was soon going crazy over the eggs, which, without exception, yielded two large yolks each. Dadu smiled at my wonderment and said Sinha Poultry, which was on the other side of the road at the point where we had got off the bus in the morning, specialized in producing double-yolk eggs. Mrinalini should take me to the poultry some time, he suggested.

Lunch over, Shibuda informed us that charpoys had been laid at the lime grove and we could rest there if we so desired. Dadu however refused, saying he would have his little siesta in his easy-chair in the sitting room. If he lay down on the charpoy he would fall fast asleep and then would have to count sheep all night. Mrinalini on her part vacillated for a few moments looking enquiringly at me, eventually made a face and said she would spend the afternoon with the books in her room. Left to myself, I fished out *Banalata Sen*, my favourite collection of poems, from my haversack and proceeded towards the clump of lime trees with a small circular clearing at the centre.

Lying on the charpoy with the book of poems unopened on my chest, I surveyed the enveloping green with patterns of azure peeking through the filigree of leaves here and there. The lime blossoms exuded a faint fragrance, as if in bashful invitation to the scores of bees and butterflies flitting around. Now and then a soft breeze blew, and with that the leaves murmured, it seemed in gentle appreciation. And at almost regular intervals, the pied crested cuckoo would call out *piu kahan* (where is my beloved?) even as the woodpecker went about methodically with its percussive *thak thak, thathak thak*. Numerous unseen birds joined in at delightfully unexpected moments to complete the music of the wilderness. It seemed it had been in my destiny to be carried one fine morning into a land where the progress of time did not mean irretrievable loss, but a soulful gain—of blessedness.

Hours had slipped away by the time Shibuda came to find out, at the behest of Dadu and Mrinalini, if I was still asleep, and if not, would I like to join them. I got up reluctantly, picked up the book that had fallen off I don't know when, and in the golden haze of the setting sun walked slowly towards my hosts savouring tea in the courtyard. Still in a daze, I slumped in a charpoy and it was only when an absent-minded sip of the blistering beverage scalded my tongue that I became fully alert.

'Hello Mr Rip Van Winkle, do we look familiar?' The complaint in Mrinalini's voice was unmistakable, but Dadu would not have me cornered.

'Had a good nap?' he intervened.

'Nap? I would never want to spoil an afternoon here sleeping.'

Dadu laughed, 'Morning shows the day, but not the evening. Hope you like the sequel too.'

We had puffed rice and brinjal fritters along with the tea as we sat there chatting in the courtyard. Gradually, the sky began to darken and Dadu said he would have to go for his evening prayers. I asked him if I could watch him pray, to which he replied, 'Why not?' And then in a conspiratorial tone he asked me, 'Do you smoke?' Rather embarrassed, I had to admit I was often guilty of the act, though I did not see what he was driving at.

'Good,' he said, 'I've observed that smokers are usually skilled at lighting incense sticks. A granddaughter of mine uses up a whole box of matchsticks to light just three—would you believe it!'

Mrinalini protested saying the number was a gross exaggeration, but when it failed to make any dent, joined us in the laughter. Dadu took me to his room and handed me a red-bordered dhoti along with a cotton stole, the traditional attire for puja.

I washed my hands and feet, this time in the in-house bathroom, put on the dhoti and wrapped the stole around my shoulders. When I emerged, Dadu looked me up from toe to head and smiled:

'Oh, you look good! I never thought you'd be able to wear that so well! You've done a pretty good job I must say. Men have forgotten how to wear our traditional dress, you know. I'm told they sell stitched dhotis in Calcutta nowadays. You can wear them like trousers. Even bridegrooms wear stitched dhotis when they go for their own wedding, just imagine!'

I told him I had been to a Ramakrishna Mission school and was used to even playing football in a dhoti.

Dadu smiled as he took out two prayer mats from the wardrobe and handing both to me led the way to the prayer room. At the entrance to the hut there stood a large broom—the kind I supposed witches used—leaning against the door frame, while next to it sat a lantern and a small pail of water. Dadu lit the lantern, and carrying it inside set it down on the smooth mud floor beside a clod of earth, which, I noted with a twitch, bore an uncanny resemblance to a porcupine that'd had all its quills pulled out and replaced by burnt-out incense sticks. Beside the porcupine, there rested on a small mat a large conch shell, plus a brass pot and a brass bell, both polished to perfection. The room lit, Dadu went to the door and hauling in the witch's broom began sweeping the spotless floor, brushing aside my offers of help. I could only watch, feeling somewhat awkward, wondering if the unlikely trinity of Shiva, Jesus on the Cross, and Hanuman looking down from their ornate frames on the wall disapproved of my conduct. My obsession with ungodly things like witches, porcupines and frogs would have already weakened my case, I rued.

The sweeping over, Dadu washed his hands at the doorstep, sprinkled some water from the brass pot on the porcupine and asked me to light three incense sticks. Then he took up the conch shell, struck it a couple of times against his palm to produce that inimitable hollow tapping sound, and blew it thrice for almost twenty long seconds in each burst. (Quite a feat for his age, I noted.)

Next, taking the incense sticks from me, he waved them at the paintings with one hand while ringing the bell with the other, finally driving the sticks into the hapless porcupine. Then he bowed before each of the pictures and whispering some lines in

Sanskrit, sat down on his prayer mat, crossing his legs in sukhasan. His eyes shut, he gestured for me to sit beside him and turned still.

I did as I was told, but a few minutes in that position and I kept turning my head to the left every now and then to see what Dadu was doing. The possibility that he might have gone off to sleep was gradually beginning to appear real. Somewhat at a loss, I was about to consider the option of getting up quietly and slipping out of the prayer room when Dadu addressed me suddenly, without turning his head and with his eyes still shut:

'I thought you'd be adept at meditation! Sit comfortably, close your eyes and observe your thoughts, like a witness. Do not get involved with them. If that is difficult, try to fix your mind on any single object, whatever that be. The idea, you know, is to still the turbulent waters of the mind. And once you've achieved stillness, you'll get a glimpse of what lies beneath.'

Startled as I was, the idea of taming a whirlpool did strike me as novel and that of fixing my mind on a single object, quite doable. I crossed my legs in padmasan, the lotus pose I had picked up early during PT classes in school, shut my eyes and decided to focus on something unique. After considering various options, I finally decided that my object of concentration, which Dadu had emphasised could be 'whatever', would be the beady-eyed frog I had spied in the dining hall.

'Frog, frog, frog, frog...' I kept repeating mentally, trying to conjure up a golden yellow image in which a plump amphibian sat pretty at the bottom of my swirling lake of consciousness. I would have gone on for five minutes or maybe a little longer when the absurdity of the whole thing began to assert itself. And with that I began to feel restless. My legs were hurting and so was my back, used to, for too long, to the comfort of a restful slouch. Every few seconds I would open my eyes only to see Dadu firmly planted in his sukhasan. Then my left elbow started itching and my right shoulder blade followed suit, but so solemn was the occasion and so complete the silence that I could not muster courage enough to so much as stir in my distressing position. 'Curiosity killed the cat!' I began rebuking myself for the needless inquisitiveness about how Dadu did his puja.

Then an idea struck me. I would engage in some mental activity in order to deflect my attention from the anatomical discomforts that were becoming increasingly acute with every passing second. I decided to count the number of quills sticking out of the porcupine, divide that by three, and then divide the quotient by two, to arrive at the number of days since the hapless animal had had its coat cleaned. The assumption being, three incense sticks were routinely stuck into it BD (bis die—a Latinism to be flaunted before Mrinalini, I noted). 'Garbage disposal inadequate,' I chuckled to myself, foretelling the conclusion that would inevitably emerge from the arithmetical exercise. Meanwhile, my legs were going numb and my back was getting sore, even as my scratch list was getting longer, now to include both my earlobes and the back of my neck.

'One, two, three…' I started counting inwardly, taking lengthy pauses between numbers. But by the time I reached fifty-six, the urge to scratch my right shoulder blade would heed no restraint even as both my legs had gone to sleep.

'Fifty-seven!' I blurted out, struck my right shoulder blade with my left paw, and by the impact of the blow first fell to my right and then quite inexplicably rolled over to lie on my back, my locked legs blooming in the air, adorned by two white lotus leaves that my rolled up dhoti had turned into.

Dadu shot up like a jack-in-the-box, was struck dumb by my impossible yogic posture, and slumped on his prayer mat convulsing in laughter.

I needed quite a bit of help to unlock my numb legs and then to be able to stand up. My embarrassment of course was beyond alleviation, although Dadu did not ask me even once how I had come to strike that unusual pose.

His only query was: 'What was that fifty-seven about?'

Benighted, Bewitched

Emerging out of the prayer room, I found myself in a completely different world. It was as dark as dark can be. Everything around seemed painted in tar, save for the windows of the bungalow, which looked like Halloween lanterns emitting an unearthly glow. The sky above, still awaiting moonrise, wore a somewhat lighter shade of black, but that made it no less sinister, given the sight it offered of dozens of wide-winged bats flying hither and thither in spooky delight above the corrugated tin roof of the ancient bungalow. The music of the wilderness that had carried me to a different land just a few hours ago had now turned decidedly sombre, what with owls screeching at the drop of a leaf and jackals howling, one on the prompt of the other, as if reciting from some macabre composition.

Dadu held my hand and guided me to the lantern-lit bungalow, where we were confronted by a curious Mrinalini awaiting to be enlightened on the strange noises coming from within the prayer room. The honours of narrating the episode were naturally bestowed on me, and I would say I made a valiant attempt at preserving my dignity to the extent that the stupidity of my tumble would allow.

The mortifying narration over, Mrinalini said Jhargram was no place to stay indoors and suggested we have tea outside, in the courtyard, the few stray mosquitoes notwithstanding. With Dadu agreeing, my say in the matter was rather limited. So, having changed into regular clothes, I trudged out again into the open.

It was not all that dark in the courtyard now. One corner of it was lit up by a hesitant lantern, which threw immense shadows all around. And on the edge, there stood a solitary mango tree on which, it seemed, the stars themselves had descended. The entire tree was lit up with fireflies, making it appear like an improbable import from the childhood land of fairies and elves. Looking up, I marvelled again, to see so many stars and constellations smiling down from regions so many light years beyond the touch of my human hands. I stood there transfixed, unable to move those few paces to the charpoy, much to the amusement of Dadu and Mrinalini.

Shibuda appeared soon with his kettle and earthen tumblers. Having served us the first round of tea, he placed the kettle at the foot of my charpoy and asked Dadu what he wanted for dinner.

'Ask our guest,' Dadu told him, upon which Shibuda looked at me.

'Anything,' I replied, not knowing what to suggest. Mrinalini came to my rescue saying chicken curry with rotis would be fine.

'Bah bah!' it seemed Shibuda was mighty pleased. 'Babu,' he now turned to Dadu, and soaping his hands at an imagined faucet made his appeal, 'it's been months since we had meat. Will you shoot a few bats for us today?'

I let out a snort almost choking on my tea, but Dadu coolly replied he would do that the next evening, after the guns had been cleaned. Shibuda appeared happy with the assurance and left with his canines twinkling. I was aghast and desperately wanted to ask Dadu if what I had heard was indeed right and whether Shibuda would actually make a meal out of the flesh, blood and

entrails of vampire bats. But before I could frame my question
in suitably inoffensive language he produced a violin from under
his charpoy and enquired if I had an ear…

'Ear! What? He eats ears too!' I was still full of ghastly
thoughts and had missed the 'for music' in Dadu's query.

Mrinalini doubled up with laughter, shrieking away to glory,
even as Dadu let out periodic grunts as he wrestled to keep his
guffaws in check.

'I asked you if you listen to music,' Dadu looked at me when
Mrinalini had got over her hysteria.

I was stumped again, not knowing what to say in reply, my
knowledge of the subject being limited to the few Hindi songs I
had picked up from movies and which our hostel superintendent
had forbidden me to sing during the admission season. Apparently,
my soulful renderings were enough to scare away even gallant
guardians, not to mention their nervous wards.

Hari darsan ki pyasi ankhiyan (These eyes thirst for a vision of
the Lord), Dadu began to the accompaniment of his mournfully
sweet violin, taking me gradually into the exquisite land of smiling
tears. And as the lines flowed out in cascades evoking before my
mind's eye heart-rending visions of a lovelorn Sree Radha pining
away for her Beloved, I found myself unable to check the tears
welling up in my eyes. The poignant wail of the violin only
added to the futility of my attempt at self restraint. Like a hare
hypnotised by the dazzle of a headlight, I sat there defenceless
beneath a canopy of gleaming stars, mesmerised by the music
that was stirring up something unknown deep within.

'Your turn now,' Dadu looked at me as he brought his recital
to a calibrated halt, ending the spell.

'No way, sir!' I cried in alarm, and again it was Mrinalini
engaging herself in the rescue act.

'Dadu, you should've been the last one to sing. But now that you have served dessert first, the dinner is spoilt.'

Dadu laughed out loud at the comment and I seized the opportunity to suggest that he tell us a story instead.

'Story,' he exclaimed, 'why I remember none! Even my grandchildren are all adults now and it's long since I read them stories.'

Not one to be discouraged so easily, I changed tack: 'It amazes me no end to think how you decided to settle down here in the middle of a forest. It must have been quite a decision.'

Dadu grew thoughtful at the remark. He looked around, taking in the acres of darkness surrounding us. Then, pouring some tea into his tumbler, he began his story:

'It was a momentous decision indeed! Young man you take me back to 1960, quite a few years before you were born, I guess. I had just lost my wife that year, to typhoid. She died after months of suffering. I immersed her ashes, as she had wished, at Prayag—the confluence of the Ganga, Yamuna and the mythical Saraswati. We were firmly settled in Allahabad at that time for quite a few generations, a whole army of relatives. Allahabad is the place I was born; it is where I obtained my college and university degrees and my job with the Indian audit department. It was there that I was initiated into Hindustani classical by some well known pandits and ustads. And Allahabad was also home to the Bengali girl I married. Initially, she was my parents' choice, later mine.

'The Chatterjees of Allahabad were known to be wealthy, I might say. But you know it is almost never the case that wealth comes alone; it arrives in pomp, with all its attendant vices. In our case the vices and the wealth had been accumulated over generations. There was rivalry, pettiness, court cases, politicking, and all the usual muck. There was affection too, I admit, but it was only the immediate family that wanted to see you happy, besides some friends of course; others were either coveting your inheritance or waiting to trap you in litigation, or generally praying for misfortune to strike you.

'I grew tired, very tired indeed. In a way, my wife was the last thread that had held me tied to Allahabad. My parents had died earlier and I had no brothers or sisters—unusual for those days when people grew football teams at home, but that was how it was. The other unusual thing was that I was the only one in the entire extended family who worked for a living. The others lived, rather thrived, on rent and lease income. The family used to own many houses, shops and markets in the city and the rents were substantial. In fact, it was this easy money that lay at the root of our perpetual feud.

'Anyway, I still had a few years left in service in 1960 when one fine morning I spotted a newspaper advertisement saying a European sahib wanted to sell off his estate at Jhargram. That was the spark! Immediately, I took a train to Calcutta and from there hired a car to Jhargram town, then got into a bullock cart and finally covered the last mile on foot. Getting to this estate on my first visit had been quite a task; the road connecting to the Bombay Highway had not been laid yet and the forest used to be much thicker then. The negotiations however went off smoothly and before leaving I paid Brown sahib the entire amount in hard cash.

'I moved into Jhargram a month later, at the peak of monsoon, having given up all claims of inheritance and property. And this is where I have lived ever since.

'Most of what you see here once belonged to Brown sahib: the bungalow, the rest of the buildings, the furniture, the cutlery, the plantation, the orchards, the framed painting of Christ in the prayer room, even Shibu Mahato. Most of the books in Mrinalini's room are also Brown's. I came in with just a few trunks, containing my clothes and some poetry. The settlement money I was paid on my premature retirement and the savings I had accumulated, I transferred to the sole bank in Jhargram town. You know, my supervisor, an Anglo-Indian gentleman, even recommended pension for me although my right to it could have been forfeited because of the early retirement.'

'But your daughters, they didn't protest?' I asked.

Dadu took a sip of the tepid tea and laughed. 'By 1960 all my daughters were married and settled, three in Calcutta and one in America. They came to know of my shift post facto. And to their credit, not one of them complained, although they would have been quite surprised I'm sure. Not even once did any of my daughters tell me that giving up all the property had been unwise; they knew how Allahabad was gnawing at my soul—all that mudslinging, backstabbing. God bless them!'

'And you too never regretted your decision?' I ventured.

'Not regretted, but on occasions initially, I did miss my friends in Allahabad, particularly Suhrid, who was quite close to me. In fact, he was the only one who knew of my whereabouts after I had fled the city of my birth.'

'He never visited you here?'

'Oh yes. Once.'

'But he didn't like the place?' I blurted out.

'No no, on the contrary, his love for this place remains immortal. In fact, he too might have been here with us this evening had providence not stood in the way.'

'Why, what happened?'

Dadu fell silent, rolling the tumbler between his palms. And as the silence lingered, I felt I had perhaps been a trifle impertinent. Not knowing how to make amends, I looked at Mrinalini only to find her staring at the mango tree. At length, Dadu smiled at me, ending my discomfiture.

'Well, as I said, Suhrid was the only one initially who knew of my escape to Jhargram. At first, he had tried to dissuade me and had even offered to fight all court cases on my behalf free of charge. He was a lawyer, and a pretty good one. But when he saw I was adamant, he relented. Suhrid was the lone man to see me off at the Allahabad railway station when I last boarded the train for Calcutta. He kept waving at me from the platform, trying to keep pace as the steam locomotive chugged away slowly, and when he had reached the end of the embankment he stood still there. I could see him wiping his tears with his handkerchief and then lost him.'

'But you said he visited you here?' I shot off a foolish query.

'Yes, but he was not lost for long,' Dadu said and continued, 'I had hardly been a month in Jhargram before a letter arrived at this address, the first letter to reach me here. It was from Suhrid. He had written to say the news of a railway station being inaugurated at Jhargram delighted him and he would visit me for a week the following month. He sought no directions, no details. He awaited no invitation. That was Suhrid!

'I was overjoyed. Shibu will tell you, so happy I was that day at receiving the letter that I had embraced him and he had rushed off to his quarters fearing the next victim would be his wife!

'Anyway, Suhrid arrived on the appointed day. I went to the station to receive him. Stepping off the train, the first thing he did was to wrap me up in his arms. He was a huge hefty fellow.

Suhrid would not let me off even as I remonstrated saying we were making quite a spectacle of ourselves there in the middle of a railway platform.

'From the station we took a bullock cart up to the point where you turn for Sinha Poultry now. There we got off and had to walk the rest of the way to the estate. The road through the village was too uneven and potholed and the forest was so dense in those days that the cart would not have made it to the bungalow. I wanted to carry Suhrid's suitcase at least half the way, but he in turn offered to carry me along with it. You know, we took one full hour and a half to cover the one mile home. Suhrid kept stopping on the way inspecting this and that and looking all around. "Wonderful", that's the only word he would utter every few minutes.'

'Wonderful!' The word just slipped out of my lips, but luckily no one paid heed.

'I was of course happy Suhrid liked the place,' Dadu resumed. 'In a way, my decision to move to this remote estate had been vindicated, not that I was looking for a certificate. Also, the apprehensions I had in my mind on whether he would be able to adjust to such basic living here were put to rest. You see, Suhrid was himself the son of a wealthy barrister and lived in a palatial house teeming with servants and valets in Allahabad.

'Once we entered the bungalow, Suhrid just collapsed with joy. He said if there was one sensible thing I had done in my entire life it was to buy this property. We had a quick breakfast, the same things that you had this morning and off he went to explore the estate. I wanted to show him around, but he said no. These things are best done alone, he insisted.'

'There was no Mrinalini then!' I smiled to myself, but made no interruption.

'Suhrid came back after an hour exhausted, but delirious with delight,' Dadu laughed. '"Chattujye," he said, "if I die before you do, bury my ashes beneath the large mahua tree at the back. I would want my soul to live here, forever. But meanwhile, there's some bad news for you." I grew apprehensive and asked him to be quick with it. "The bad news is," he said, "I've decided to live here with you, till I kick the bucket."'

Dadu paused and turning his eyes away from me said, 'But that was not to be. Suhrid died in a train accident on his way back to Allahabad.'

'Oh my god!' I sat up on the charpoy.

A strange silence descended as Dadu looked away. It seemed the mango tree, lit up here and there with fireflies, would soon be snuffed out by the clammy breath of the surrounding darkness.

'Suhrid's ashes lie beneath the mahua tree behind the bungalow,' he sighed at length, and a wave of grief appearing from nowhere swept over me.

I kept quiet, and so did Mrinalini. There was nothing to be said. The three of us sat there silent in the darkness, beneath a star-studded sky, our eyes fixed on the iridescent mango tree. Time passed us by, leaving each one of us to our private heartaches. When I awoke to the world around me, I realized that nature herself had turned softer too. The zephyr that caressed us, the occasional hoot of the owl, the mournful howl of the jackals, the soft rustle of leaves—every element of nature, it seemed, was straining to reach out to us, to comfort us, share our anguish. Startling myself as much as the others I gave away my chain of thought: 'It is we who give the world around us its identity.'

Dadu took his eyes off the mango tree and looked at me. And as I lowered my head, embarrassed at the inappropriateness of my abrupt declaration, he spoke out slowly:

'*It was dark when we approached Sicily, and against the sunset sky, Etna was in slight eruption. As we entered the straits of Messina, the moon rose, and I walked up and down the deck beside the Swami, while he dwelt on the fact that beauty is not external, but already in the mind. On one side frowned the dark crags of the Italian coast, on the other, the island was touched with silver light. "Messina must thank me," he said, "it is I who give her all her beauty."*

'You went to a Ramakrishna Mission school—do you know where that is from? From Sister Nivedita's Diary. The "Swami" is Swami Vivekananda. But you must be knowing all that.'

I nodded.

'Yet death is not the end of life,' Dadu remarked all of a sudden, and I straightened, my ears pricked up. 'Desires survive death. And all desires must perforce be fulfilled. As Bhagavan Buddha said, there's no escape from the cycle as long as one has desires. One must take birth again and again till such time that the taste for these desires is extinguished, rather rendered worthless, by the experience of the highest pleasure—of union, yoga. It's like a child who will not give up her rag doll come what may, but later having experienced greater pleasures only laughs when shown the rag she once would not part with. In Suhrid's case, he remains in love with Jhargram. He still visits this place.'

It was as if I had been struck by a thunderclap.

'Wha...what do you mean?' my feeble voice queried.

'I know it's unusual. I too didn't know of it for long.'

'And then?'

~

My tone must have had something in it. Dadu ran his fingers through his hair and continued: 'About a year or so after the train accident, it was mango season then, and I was fast asleep in my room. It was quite late into the night when I was woken suddenly by noises coming from the orchard. The mangoes were almost ripe, and that is the time when the Lodhas descend on orchards. The Lodhas are one of the tribes here who hunt and collect forest produce for a living. They come with their women and children and clean up the whole place in minutes. I hollered for Shibu who yelled back and in the next instant both of us were out here in the courtyard. I had my double barrel with me, but wasn't certain if it would be wise to pursue the Lodhas. If any of them got hurt they would just shoot at us with their poisoned arrows. So what I did was to fire a few shots in the air. That did the trick! In a flash the Lodhas were out, trampling the hedge and jumping over. After waiting for some time, Shibu and I walked up to the gate and there I fired a few more shots.

'But as we walked back from the gate, with Shibu ahead of me showing the way with the lantern, my eyes fell on the mahua tree behind the bungalow. It seemed there was somebody sitting there leaning against the tree looking skyward with his chin resting on one hand. I cocked my gun and kept following Shibu silently, who was obviously watching only the path ahead. And as we drew closer to the bungalow, the figure became clearer. The man was dressed in a white dhoti-kurta and appeared to be staring at the sickle moon overhead. A few more paces and my heart froze. It was Suhrid!'

My heart raced and I turned to Mrinalini on instinct, but she was too far gone within her shell to come to my rescue this time. And here was Dadu going on as if it was a most ordinary tale in the world.

'I controlled myself quickly,' Dadu continued. 'I did not utter a word and just shut the door as I got into the bungalow. Shibu, not having seen what I had, went off to his quarters.

'I could not sleep that night. But neither would I go out and investigate. Not even with Shibu by my side. The turmoil continued for days. "Was it just a hallucination, or was it actually Suhrid?" But as weeks passed, I came to gradually convince myself that what I had seen was my imagination projected onto an image, just as it happens so often in dreams. And having acquired the comfort of a rational explanation, my fear subsided and I would go out again in the night, often up to the mahua tree.'

I was about to pose a question when Dadu resumed. 'Suhrid appeared again one night, at the same place and sitting the same way. I got scared this time too, but not as much as on the first occasion. What I did then was to watch him from the safety of distance. He never moved, just kept staring skyward.

'The next night however, he did not appear, and again I began to doubt my previous night's experience. A few months passed, and all of a sudden I saw him again, sitting beneath the same mahua tree and in the same posture.

'This went on for quite some time until I was convinced that what I saw was real. He remains there until I'm about five or six feet away from him, but if I go any closer, he gets up and leaves. I've never seen his full face, just one side of it. And from that angle he looks exactly the same as I saw him for the last time here in Jhargram.'

Dadu paused, allowing me to heave a secret sigh. But the very next moment Mrinalini, in an unpardonable act of stupidity, cleared her throat and I almost jumped out of my skin.

'What timing!' I gnashed my teeth and was promptly punished by Dadu's ominous query:

'Have you noticed the seat at the base of the large mahua tree at the back?'

I could only nod.

'I had it built for him,' the unsuspecting gentleman went on. 'Since the day it was made, Suhrid has been using it whenever he comes. I believe he reciprocates my feelings, but for some reason I may never know, he does not ever come to me. And neither does he appear anywhere other than at the base of the mahua. He remains his own master; just as he was in life. He will not come if I call him. He appears only when he wants to. All I am allowed to do is watch him. He does not respond to my whispers. But yes, when I play the violin for him he stays as long as I have not finished. But finish I must before the sky turns pale for sunrise...'

'Babu, the food is getting cold,' Shibuda's reassuring voice brought us back to the everyday world. It was quite late already and there was no point keeping the Mahato family waiting.

~

The dinner happened in thoughtful silence and before I knew what I was eating, it was over. As we emerged from the dining hall, Dadu asked me if it was all right if Shibuda made my bed in the room adjoining his and I said yes.

'If you want I will ask Shibu or one of his sons to sleep in your room tonight,' Dadu suggested, but I dismissed the proposal with a foolish laugh.

'Cigarette?' the elderly gentleman popped the question all of a sudden as we got into the bungalow and I was aghast. So was Mrinalini.

'No sir!' I replied, embarrassed.

But Dadu waved my protestation aside, 'I have a carton of JPS that my son-in-law, Mrinalini's father, gifted me the last time he came here. Among all foreign brands, John Players Special has a special place in my taste buds, shall we say. I share it only with sinners I like.'

I looked at Mrinalini and she winked, which meant I could go ahead.

'All right sir, if you insist,' I mumbled, feeling very pleased.

Dadu went to his room and brought a packet of JPS along with an exquisite crystal ashtray.

'Brown's,' he said as he caught me admiring it. We went out again to sit under the stars, my back to the mahua behind the bungalow.

'Smoking is bad, no doubt,' Dadu opened the conversation after we had lit our cigarettes, 'but if you are not a slave to the habit and smoke once in a while, the body can easily neutralize its harmful effects.'

'If you know it's harmful why have it in the first place?' Mrinalini argued with conviction.

'Sometimes a little harm can do a lot of good as well; the collateral benefits of friendly fire, you could say,' Dadu smiled. 'Take the present case, for instance: smoking together with your friend, I would say, is a more efficient way of conveying to him the message that he is from now on my friend as well. If I were only to use words to express the same feeling, I'm not sure the impact would be the same. In fact, there is a possibility I would be taken as a sentimental fogey, more emotional than sincere.'

Mrinalini burst out laughing and said, 'I hate Geminis! Dadu, you know, you sometimes remind me of Henry in *The Picture of Dorian Gray*.'

'And what do you think of Oscar Wilde?' posed Dadu.

'Oh, too good!' Mrinalini cooed, but was on her guard immediately, 'Don't tell me he was a Gemini!'

'Well, if a Vedic astrologer were to cast Oscar Wilde's horoscope, I'm sure he would have found him a native of Mithun rashi, the Indian equivalent of the sun sign Gemini. But according to the Western system, which is generally accepted as not being as accurate as ours, I think Oscar would be a wild Libran.'

'Oh stop it, Dadu!' Mrinalini laughed. And I joined in, relieved that the conversation had nothing to do with the other-worldly.

Smoking over, we left the courtyard on a happy note. My hosts went off to their respective rooms and I got into mine. Having changed into pyjamas I entered the mosquito net and then pushing out a tentacle like an octopus, tried to dim the lantern on the table. But the lantern simply went out, and before I could even blink the world around me was plunged in darkness. The sole object visible in the room was the open window and the view it offered was far from comforting: dark swaying silhouettes of countless trees, vampire bats flying across the weirdly-lit sky, and fireflies dancing about in some necrolatrous ceremony.

What if Suhridbabu comes? The moment the possibility arose in my mind, paralysis struck my limbs. Maybe he would want to take a peek at me from the window. Why is it that Dadu had never seen his full face? Maybe a part of it had been disfigured in the accident. Oh, why did I not let Shibuda's son sleep in this room? Why couldn't I stop making a fool of myself all the time? It was quite likely Suhridbabu would resent my presence in the estate, especially now that I knew his story. Maybe this was the room he had thought he would occupy once he had shifted to Jhargram. Ideas ghastly and sickening raced fiercely one on the heel of the other even as I sat petrified on the bed like a stunned octopus with its extended tentacle frozen stiff.

It is all very likely I would have given up the ghost in the next few moments but for Shibuda's voice, which quite unexpectedly broke the stifling stillness of the night. He was calling out for his little son. But to me it meant he was awake and just a scream away. Slowly, my blood began to thaw and resumed its flow. I discovered afresh I could move my limbs in the directions I wanted and the first thing I did was to withdraw my hand into the mosquito net. Then I peeled off the bed sheet from the mattress and covering myself with it from head to toe, lay still on the bed. It was quite warm, but who cared? I would not open my eyes to anything in the world before it was morning.

It would have been some twenty minutes or so in the suffocating wrap of the bed sheet when my ears picked up the sound of violin first and then Dadu's mellifluous voice wafting in through the open window. *Ghoonghat ke pat khol re tohe piya milenge*...went the lyric as I crept out from under the bed sheet and gradually lost myself in the world of musical petition. 'Lift your veil and you will behold the Beloved', he wove the words in myriad notes as I sat still, hooked yet again.

By the time the first song was over, I had gained strength enough to get off the bed and move closer to the window. Soon, Dadu began *Chalo man Ganga Jamuna teer*... And the call to the blessed banks of the sacred rivers would suffer no resistance. Quietly unbolting the door that opened to the side of the bungalow, I began following the trail of the violin, and before I knew it, the large mahua tree stood directly in front of me.

My limbs froze. I was too scared to go either way. Neither could I move closer to Dadu, nor return to my room; my feet just wouldn't move. But as the songs flowed, my fears ebbed and moving behind a sal trunk I watched the old gentleman sitting on a small straw mat offer one song after another apparently to the cement seat at the foot of the tree. A violin in hand, a gun on one side and a flickering lantern on the other, he went on with his touching performance, unaware that I stood watching just a few yards behind him.

An hour would have passed when it seemed Dadu would end his recital soon. Lest my intrusion be detected, I quickly returned to my room and silently bolted the door only to be confronted at once by the same stifling darkness that was about to choke me a little while ago. Like a blind man I groped about for some time and finally having located the bed got into the safety of the mosquito net. Tucking in the net closely I made the silent resolution that never would I allow myself to get so scared again.

'*Never*,' I repeated with emphasis and rested my head on the pillow just as someone descended on the corrugated tin roof above with a thud. Instantly, several unseen feet began running helter skelter across the false ceiling just a few feet above me, throwing the night out of gear all over again. I sat bolt upright, the bed creaked, and everything stopped just as suddenly as it had begun. I remained still for some time, sweating profusely, then began moving my hand ever so slowly towards the pillow behind me. The only thing I could do, I thought, was to spring out of the bed, cover the face of my befuddled adversary—if it had one at all (Oh Lord!)—with the pillow and throwing him to the ground, smother him to death. But everything was silent again. I sat stock-still, ears cocked, eyes wide open and my body a coil of muscles wound stiff and ready to strike at anything that moved within my reach.

Nothing happened. Not a stir. But as I rolled my eyeballs to inspect the corners of the room, I found the walls moving gradually closer and closer towards me. I was in sheer panic and tried to scream but my throat had given up.

I do not know what happened next, but when I opened my eyes the sky was bright and cheerful and the window pane reflected the trees not in black and white but in brilliant shades of green. Soon I could hear Dadu calling out for Shibuda and got out of bed. I stepped into the courtyard and to my surprise found Mrinalini returning from her morning walk, a bamboo stick in hand and a halo around her head.

'Hey sleepy head, good morning! Slept well?' she beamed.

'Good morning,' I evaded a reply.

'You must be pretty brave, Dadu was saying. Nobody sleeps well the first night here, you know, and that too for so long.'

'Why, is the house haunted?' I asked casually, simulating unconcern.

'To first-time visitors it appears so, what with owls and bats descending on the tin roof and mice running across the wooden beams of the false ceiling. Besides, it's pretty warm this time of the year and we don't have fans—it couldn't have been too comfortable, could it?'

'Good morning young man,' Dadu joined us, his face lit up by a smile. 'I was just telling Mrinalini you're quite a brave person. You put out the lantern and just went off to sleep as if you had been living here for ages.'

'Good morning sir. But how do you know I put out the lantern?'

'I saw the light go out. I could see you put out the light because you had left the connecting door ajar, which again surprised me.'

'Oh, did I? And I changed into pyjamas with the door open!' I went red all over.

'Well there were no witnesses to that, I assure you,' Dadu sought to comfort me even as Mrinalini fought to suppress a smile.

I kept silent for some time but finally decided to come out with the truth.

'Actually,' I said, 'last night could well have been the last in my life. I had put out the lantern by accident and out of the ten hours I'd have slept, at least eight would have been spent senseless. I was so terribly scared that I just passed out.'

Dadu and Mrinalini were in splits. I had little choice but to join in and Shibuda, appearing with his kettle and tumblers, began laughing too, without of course knowing in the least what the joke was all about.

'What do you think of my outdoor loo?' Dadu asked, pouring tea into the earthen cups even as I debated within whether to have the tea first and then brush my teeth as I did at Hindu Hostel, or the other way round.

'I would say it's almost perfect,' I said, deciding to brush later.

'A ceiling would have made it perfect, you mean?'

'No, you should've had a fig tree instead of a neem.'

Dadu patted my back and laughed as Mrinalini gave me a thumbs-up, saying Geminis could be rather entertaining once in a while. Presently, Shibuda arrived announcing breakfast.

I looked at Dadu's old HMT Janata. It was 10.40, exactly 24 hours since my arrival in Jhargram.

~

I spent the next thirteen days at Dadu's estate, exploring it and the forest beyond, listening to stories and recitals, learning to shoot bats in the dark by aiming at their gleaming eyes, and reading strange books, among them *Bardo Thodol* (the Tibetan Book of the Dead) in translation. I visited Sinha Poultry with my cheerful guide to look up fat hens that never failed to lay double-yolk eggs, Mothurbabu and family in their koalaic habitat of eucalyptus trees, Shibuda's quaint village with mud huts and straw roofs, and a few places of tourist interest nearby, like the ancient Kanak Durga temple beside a meandering stream.

And almost every morning, before the drops of dew on the wild grass, the dancing flowers and the nodding leaves had returned to the hidden vaults of the other paradise, I would be out with Mrinalini, amidst the glorious burst of foliage within the estate, or outside, along the banks of the prattling canal, holding hands, or arm in arm, gazing perhaps at the crimson horizon in the distance, or at the emerald forest on either flank coming into radiance, whispering sweet nothings into an acquiescing ear, wrapping my fingers around a soft melting fist, or thanking the unseen stars for some wanton windfall: the occasion to rescue a fluttering sleeve from an ambush of thorns, or to hold, for an eternity or two, the soft contours of the beloved's fragrant being in an astonished embrace as she tripped over some impish stone.

My first visit to Jhargram was followed by several others, mostly at Mrinalini's invitation or Dadu's. It is the place where I first discovered what a raw cashew nut looks like, clinging onto an apple-like fruit hanging from a small tree. Jhargram is the place I learnt to decipher the secrets of the weather by interpreting cloud formations, by noting the distance between the moon and the rings encircling it, by the movement of ants shifting residence from one corner to another with their eggs held aloft in tiny pincers. My acquaintance with the various stars and constellations

I owe to Jhargram, and my preference for the Bangla 'Kaalpurush' over the Greek-derived Orion to Dadu. And yes, Shibuda is the person who taught me how to tap honey from a hive without getting stung by the bees and hold a drink of fermented mahua without losing respectability.

The wonders of a forest town apart, Jhargram is also the place where I first awoke to the assurance of a private cosmos, one in which the beloved always revolved close in a small orbit, sometimes appearing before my bewitched eyes in full radiance, showering a dazzling smile or gifting a gentle caress, and sometimes remaining invisible, sending out waves of delicate fragrance perhaps from amidst a pile of hoary books or a riot of sun-drenched leaves, holding me entranced even in absentia.

I would not risk that assurance, even at the pain of hanging, in the crafty pursuit of any fleeting, furtive, corporal gratification, certain as I was that eternity lurked in the wings. An eternity that held within its infinite arms the promise of countless pulsating moments in which the last fabric of a hindrance between the two of us would be flung aside, making way for the rapturous consummation of a never-ending romance.

Over the years, I heard many stories from Dadu and met quite a few of his friends at Jhargram. One person who Dadu said I should have certainly met was Alfred Chamrette.

'Chamrette was great company,' Dadu once told me. 'A few years my junior, he remained a busy bee till he died. After his family left him, he was distraught for some time, but recovered pretty soon. 'I don't let the evening get me down' was his favourite line from an old song. We often talked about writing about each other's lives some day, you know. We were that close...'

'But you can still write about his life,' I had suggested, also telling Dadu that I had long adopted Mr Chamrette's favourite line as a sort of motto, something to be mastered over time. He had laughed and said—it had then seemed to me in jest—he would much rather write my story.

'You and your Ghosh Jethu will make an excellent account,' he would often say in his later years, his smile hinting at the mysterious.

The Last Handshake

Long had been the years since I had last visited Jhargram or met Dadu in person. It is not that the land of sal, mahogany, mehul and cashew had lost its charm, or that I had grown weary of the owner of the faraway forest estate—far from it. It is only that visiting Dadu would have complicated matters further. But I wrote to him frequently, keeping him informed of the changes in my situation, the imprints the intervening events had left behind and the upheavals they had caused. The arrangement, I well knew, could not continue forever, and so did it end one summer day in June. A little less than twenty years since Mrinalini had first walked into her grandpa's reclusive forest estate with me bumbling at her heels.

It was a routine day at Bengal Renaissance College: garrulous students, stolid professors, smelly washrooms, quiet library, the occasional clang of tramcars ferrying passengers across the pedagogic expanse of College Street, and the exhausted blue of a summer noon peeping in through the cracked atrium of the college building. The rhythm was broken all of a sudden by a rushing peon who almost collided with me at the landing between two flights of stairs to say that he had placed on hold an urgent telephone call for me at the principal's office. I followed the fleet-footed messenger hurriedly into the (thankfully) empty office of my senior colleague and was taken aback when the stern voice at the other end introduced herself as Mrinalini's mother.

The lady, about whom I had heard much but somehow never met, said her father—Mrinalini's grandpa—had taken ill at Jhargram and that he had been brought over to their Shyambazar home for treatment. The old gentleman had expressed his desire to see me, the sooner the better. I was shocked, but even so enquired after Mrinalini out of courtesy. There was a long silence at the other end, after which I was informed in a rather curt voice that Mrinalini was abroad at her aunt's and had been unable to advance her return before the day following the next.

That afternoon, carrying with me two of Dadu's favourites, potato chips and soan papri, both picked up hurriedly from the college canteen, I arrived at Mrinalini's parental home in Shyambazar in a taxi. A boy servant with curious eyes answered the hysterical doorbell, an oddity in the ancient house, and guided me through the courtyard and then through what appeared to be the dining room into a large bedroom that had all the curtains drawn. For a few seconds the darkness got me fumbling, but I could soon see Dadu, who I had not met in several years, stretched on an ancient four-poster with two large pillows tucked under his head. He turned towards me as I cleared my throat politely to announce my arrival and welcomed me with a smile, which still comes back to me after all these years to salve my moments of loneliness. He could neither have the chips nor the sweets, but seemed very pleased that I had remembered his birthday even in the hurry.

I spent the entire afternoon with Dadu, telling him of my lecturing job, my folks at Ranchi, the books I had read recently (among them the Omar Sharif co-authored *Goren's Bridge Complete*, which Dadu had recommended to me long back noticing my poor bridge game), the plays I had seen during the past few months and so on. He listened attentively and every now and then smiled as if to say my company pleased him.

Then, all of a sudden, raising his head slightly he asked me in a very weak voice about my present marital status. I told him I was still not formally divorced although Sraboni had not visited me even once since hastening off in a huff to her parents' place ages back—about which he already knew from my long stream-of-consciousness outpourings contained in thick stamped envelopes—and that I had no intentions of marrying again. He next enquired after my daughter Titir, and for a moment I was lost for words. She was doing fine, I said in the end, taking care not to distress him with the complexity of my emotion towards my only child: I did miss her occasionally, with longing sometimes, but had been unable to get over my unspoken reluctance at bringing into a random world a child who would always remain a proxy.

'Marriage as an institution appears to be falling apart in these godless times,' Dadu commented at length sinking back into the bed and mumbled something about Mrinalini going through a bad patch trying to evade her destiny.

I showed no curiosity.

We remained silent, a feeling of awkwardness slowly creeping up, but order was soon restored as the little fellow with the curious eyes walked in with a large crystal tray, followed by Mrinalini's mother. A mug of tea and a plate full of assorted cookies were on offer, and I was asked to help myself.

I got up to greet Mrinalini's mother, earning myself half a nod by way of acknowledgement, and then picked up the mug and a cookie out of sheer politeness.

The mother I noticed was a rotund figure, her considerable height squared off by an equally generous girth, and her face sporting large watery eyes, an aquiline nose and a thin mouth that curved down abruptly at both ends to give her an expression of total aloofness. With her commanding presence, she appeared to me to be some kind of a retired empress, who in her growing years had been taught to be polite and considerate to the less fortunate, but still needed some effort to play that role. And I was aghast, when, with Dadu in full hearing, she said her father had been harbouring prostate cancer for long in blissful ignorance and had now reached a stage well beyond chemotherapy. Then, after a pause, she added God had however been kind to him and had to be thanked for sparing him the pain the ailment usually caused when metastasizing.

Two drops of tear, overcoming the will of their hapless owner, rolled down my cheeks, one falling right into the mug I was holding. That caught her eye, bringing about a sudden and inexplicable change in her confident demeanour. Bursting into tears, she hurried out of the room leaving with me the words that could well have been mine:

'He deserves all the kindness in the world... He has been so kind himself...'

Struggling to stifle my sobs, I kept staring at the mug of tea that my right hand held in its trembling grip even as the left one clutched at a shaking cookie. After a while, when the tremors had subsided, I looked up at Dadu, only to see him gazing at me with a faint smile—a smile that could only have been brought to blossom by the benevolent design of an empathetic heart.

Left alone facing an irretrievable Dadu and with the shadow of imminent parting lurking within the opulent folds of the heavy floral curtains that, ironically, held at bay the radiant exuberance of the tropical summer afternoon outside, I was at a complete loss, not knowing what to do or say. I kept staring at the carved headboard of the four-poster, against which, intermittently, the worn out dust jacket of the funerary *Bardo Thodol* would suddenly appear and trail away even as I fought to convince myself that I had been mistaken: the angel of death stood not at the threshold but was a long way off. The old gentleman seemed to have read my thoughts.

'*Sunset and evening star,*
And one clear call for me!
And may there be no moaning of the bar,
When I put out to sea...' he recited faintly, and then turning his head away from me posed a strange question: 'But where does *your* story end, Baba?'

I did not know how to answer that and said so.

Dadu smiled and his halting words only deepened the mystery: 'In *Poetics*, Aristotle says the plot must be a whole, with a beginning, middle and end... The plot of your life, as far as I have understood it and written about, is clear till the intermission...the middle of the middle, one might say... I wish you would take it up from where I left and complete it...your way. Will you do that, Baba?'

I would have sought clarifications, but noticing that a conversation would only drain Dadu further, I pulled up my chair close to the bed and began stroking his frail arm, punctured at several spots presumably for blood samples, as he kept his eyes closed.

Eventually, when the little fellow came in to switch on the lights in the room and tell us that the doctor was on his way, I got up rather reluctantly and told Dadu I had better leave. The old gentleman made quite an effort and extended his feeble hand towards me. Instinctively I went down on my knees and lowered my head for him to touch and bless. Dadu gave me his blessings, then gestured for me to hold his hand.

That was the last handshake. On the fourteenth of June. His birthday and mine.

~

For quite some months since then, memories of Jhargram besieged me all the time, showing scant regard for the place I was in, the people I was with, or the truckloads of work that had been dumped on me. Try as I might, I would not believe that lost forever was the old man I had loved, and his quiet forest estate, which would never have turned me away in my moment of anguish and loneliness if I ever sought refuge. It gave me no solace to reason Shibuda was still there as the caretaker and would perhaps take me in on a dark rainy night, if I stood drenched and hesitant at the rickety bamboo gate—once the gateway to the only paradise I have known.

I buried myself in work, reading, taking down notes, attending seminars, visiting public libraries and generally keeping myself stationed at the desiccated level of the intellect, lest the deluge of emotions swelling and crashing underneath sweep me away. Returning to my lonely apartment—the Banerjees, with the plural 's' clearly inappropriate since long—after the day's work had become a nightmare. I would get back late in the night, open the door and just stand there, the darkness bringing back memories of Jhargram in surges.

The Black Box

With the passing on of Dadu, I had initially tried to convince myself that the sounds and the echoes of Jhargram and everything associated with them would by and by retreat into the ever-receding world of fading reverberations, like the peal of a ponderous brass bell, suspended at the entrance of some ancient Himalayan temple, that at first startles, then lingers, and finally withdraws into the hollows of the stretching infinite. But Jhargram never ended with Dadu, as I was to discover, again on a working day, barely a year after the old gentleman's death, from a roll of paper spouting out of a noisy news ticker.

But before the fire, the ice: my frigid situation at Bengal Renaissance College, where I was a lecturer. The college had been mulling an undergraduate course in journalism for some time and was then looking for faculty, when one day I was summoned by the somewhat eccentric principal, Dr Ashim Baran Chanda (ABCD in student circles, the D having been drafted in from the surname and uppercased as a joke), who had at one time published a handful of controversial papers on the fourteenth-century Maithili poet Vidyapati to tepid in-house applause.

'Mr Banerjee, you once worked for a newspaper, right?'

'Not a newspaper, sir a business fortnightly.'

'It's all the same.'

The principal fidgeted with his fancy dip pen for some time and worked himself up into a sort of challenging assertiveness, knitting his bushy eyebrows into an intimidating frown.

'Do you know Vidyapati wrote on law?'

'No sir,' I confessed, adding, 'I thought he wrote only love poems, religious love I mean.'

My answer appeared to satisfy the odd academic. Smiling somewhat sarcastically, he mumbled, 'Religious love, bhakti, prem, rubbish! As if by changing the label, you can change the content!' He paused for the aside to sink in and resumed: 'You know, at one time, even I did not know Vidyapati wrote on law, or for that matter on ethics, history, geography… But when I got to know Maithil Kavi Kokil also wrote on law, I began my research. You see, I can trace my family on my mother's side to a person who was very close to the famous Rash Behari Ghose, the top lawyer at the Calcutta High Court during British times in the late 1800s. There is some law running in my veins along with literature, if I may say so. Anyway, you can see for yourself the fruits of my diligent research: my position, peer respect…'

I did not quite get what he was hinting at, and waited for him to establish the link.

'You may not know much about journalism, because you have never worked for a daily paper. Fine, but what prevents you from getting into research? Why can't you take a few classes every week if we start the journalism course? Just read up, research, and distribute your knowledge among students. In any case you read the newspaper every day I hope.'

It was clear I had no choice.

Reeling under the imposition, I turned up that evening at the house of Paranjoy Guha, once a fellow student, then a professor of English at a south Calcutta college, and always a person full of practical wisdom. He welcomed me with open arms, said he could offer no snacks along with the rum and cola since his 'family' was not around, and complained that I had not kept in touch with him since my transfer from Delhi to Calcutta. The prelims over, he listened to my tale of woe almost absent-mindedly, cleaning a camera lens with a tattered vest all the while. Then, cutting my rant short, he asked:

'Do you remember Cleopatra?'

'Who would forget him!'

'Do you know what he does now?'

I said the last time I had heard of Cleopatra, he was some bigwig at the Zoological Survey of India shuttling between the Eastern Himalayas and the Western Ghats, but that was ages ago.

'Well Cleopatra has shifted his focus from faunal diversity to feminine singularity. He now runs an NGO that is seeking, with great success, to popularize the use of sanitary napkins among womenfolk in the backward villages of West Bengal.'

I could only gape at Paranjoy, the glass of rum and cola frozen midair.

'Sudipto, what is it that makes you so apprehensive?' Paranjoy now seemed serious. 'You were once a journalist and a technical editor as well. If Cleopatra can find true bliss in a sanitary towel, why can't you in a newspaper or a toilet paper, whatever it is?'

I found the link between a hygiene product and the alleged allotropes of paper a bit tenuous, but got the message nonetheless.

In time, Bengal Renaissance College launched its course in journalism and as part of the 'practicals' started an in-house weekly newspaper, *Bengal Renaissance*, of which I was nominated the deputy editor. It was a full team, complete with an editor (ABCD), a deputy editor, a news editor, a chief of news bureau, a chief sub-editor, a chief reporter, several sub-editors, and as many reporters. Except for the first two, all were undergraduate students and their roles were interchangeable. About two hundred copies of the newspaper were printed every Thursday night and circulated among the students and faculty of the college at the end of Friday's classes. I do not know what use the readers put the paper to over the weekend.

The publishing setup was quite elaborate and modern, with one large heavy-duty printer, several personal computers, a scanner, a facsimile machine, a photocopier and a teleprinter. The college subscribed to the services of Press Trust of India, the news agency, which fed it with ceaseless cascades of news reports throughout the day and night.

For some time I remained aloof, not being very enthusiastic about my deputy editor's role as it was excruciatingly boring, but soon figured a way out. Having convinced ABCD that a hands-on demonstration of how to edit copy, craft headlines that fitted the various column widths (with my obscure knowledge of picas and points) and do layouts would be more instructional for students, I joined the team as a 'consulting deputy editor', a designation that ABCD took pride in having invented. The students relished this, and I was relieved too, hoping secretly that watching me edit copy and provide headlines they would be persuaded eventually to treat my name with greater kindness.

For considerable time my professional and personal lives ran along parallel tracks, until they converged one fateful evening, without warning.

One late Thursday at the college press, as I stood guard at the ticker on the request of the student chief sub who was busy putting the edition to bed, I had the strange feeling that something was amiss. As the feeling grew the ticker came to life and in its typical staccato style spewed out a report with the headline 'Forest

Fire at Jhargram'. I snatched the copy from the machine and raced through it at one breath. The fire, presumably the handiwork of some local extremist elements, had not only burnt down much of the forest, but consumed some old British-era bungalows at Garh Salboni as well.

The chief sub hollered 'Page one news, sir?' from the other end of the room.

'Single column... No, briefs, first item,' I hollered back and sank into the chair nearby.

'I'm going to Jhargram to your grandpa's by the six o'clock Ispat Express tomorrow morning. There's been a fire at Salboni, just got it from PTI,' I fancied calling up Mrinalini from some telephone.

'Good Lord! I'll join you at the station,' would perhaps have been her reply.

The next morning I took the 6.15 Ispat from Howrah. And about three hours later there I was standing on the railway platform at Jhargram. Soon I got into a true-to-memory public bus, along with a crowd of men, women, poultry and goats. The wheezing and clanking vehicle dropped me at Sinha Poultry, from where I walked to the devastated estate through a still smouldering land that was once a forest, deaf to the advice and protestations of the forest officials and police constables swarming the place.

Dadu's entire estate had been destroyed, along with those of Mothurbabu, Mr Chamrette and all others along the line, right up to the clearing of Ledhabera, which was an unexpectedly open area without trees or shrubs on one side of the forest. I walked into what had once been the land of my awakening, trampling on the remains of the burnt out bamboo gate and was soon joined by a weeping Shibuda, now quite aged but still with black hair, and his family. Mothurbabu, all grey now, also came in a little later, misty eyed and accompanied by his wife who walked with a stick, and two stoical sons. There was nothing much to salvage, except for some disfigured metal utensils and some pieces of cutlery. But as I entered the heap that was once Dadu's room, I noticed something like a box with patches of orange, peeping from beneath the smouldering logs that once held up the corrugated tin roof of the bungalow.

Taking out my handkerchief I had just bent down to pick up the blackened box, when an imperious voice asked me not to touch it. Turning around, I was taken aback to find Mrinalini's mother standing behind me, in the company of a tall, wiry man who appeared to be her driver.

I moved back, allowing the putative driver to step in and make an attempt at picking up the tin suitcase. He tried to grasp it with both hands and in the next instant jumped up blowing and spitting on his palms and letting out a string of expletives in his native Hindi. Then noticing his lady employer glaring at him, he was so embarrassed that he began mumbling strange words that sounded like some magic chant. This infuriated Mrinalini's mother further, and she thundered, 'Stop it! Ram Singh, stop behaving like a possessed woman! Go, get the duster from the car and keep this box in the dicky.'

It was now my turn to be spoken to.

'How did you get to know of the fire?' the former empress demanded.

'From a PTI take.'

'PTI? Take? What language are you talking in?'

'I meant from Press Trust of India, the news agency. The college I teach at subscribes to PTI, and I got the news from a report they sent us.'

'And you didn't inform us?'

'I have not kept your numbers.'

'I see,' the lady appeared convinced after some initial dithering. Softening her tone, she said, 'I know you loved Baba. He too had great affection for you.'

The abrupt words of kindness caught me off guard and I did not know how to react. The smouldering debris of the bungalow, once the home of an old man I had loved, lay sprawling before my smarting eyes, even as the sleepy secluded estate beyond stood devastated. The estate that had once awakened me to the world of majestic trees, whispering shadows, evocative fragrances and lingering silences, punctuated by birdsong. The estate that had once presented before me the possibility of an eternity holding within its infinite arms countless blissful moments with Mrinalini.

I stood still, staring at the destruction close at my feet, my unseeing eyes playing back scenes from an innocent past: the moon throwing a silvery diaphanous veil over the sprawling estate late into a fragrant night; the red murram path leading to the bamboo gate unfurling like a maiden's ribbon at the feet of the lofty sals; the fairytale mango tree shimmering at the edge of the courtyard, lit up with fireflies; Dadu's mournfully sweet violin carrying me ever so softly into the exquisite land of smiling tears; Mrinalini's chiselled face, mysterious, bewitching, peering through the pattern of obovate moon-dusted cashew leaves...

'Mohenjo Daro, the Mound of the Dead,' a teasing voice whispered, and as I turned around startled, I found Mrinalini's mother staring at me, her eyes brimming with tears and her mouth covered with the end of her sari.

'God bless you,' she stifled a sob and swiftly went off in the direction of the ruined orchard. Soon afterwards, Ram Singh, the driver, came in with a large cloth duster, picked up the half-burnt suitcase and left for the car, parked somewhere on the other side of the main road, near Sinha Poultry, I presumed.

I stayed for some time and then decided to get moving; there was no point hanging around.

~

A few months had passed since my impulsive visit to Jhargram when I was accosted once again in college, by the same hurrying peon who even this time had an identical message to deliver: a telephone call awaited my answer at the principal's office.

The voice this time was softer. Mrinalini's mother asked me to read out my address slowly so that she could note it down and added she would send Ram Singh to my place to hand over 'something' Dadu had left for me. I did not ask what the 'something' was.

When I returned home late that evening, I found Ram Singh pacing at the staircase. He appeared greatly relieved to see me and running to the car parked at the gate of the apartment complex brought out a large carton, holding it as if it were a child. He said he had instructions not to deliver the 'packet' to anyone other than me, even if that meant awaiting my return till midnight. I tipped Ram Singh, much to his surprised delight, told him I too lived in Bihar once upon a time long, long ago, and carried the rather heavy carton upstairs to the Banerjees.

Setting the liberally scotchtaped carton on the cane centre table in the small drawing room of my flat, I pulled up a chair close, little knowing that what would emerge from the box was the singed tin suitcase that had once been orange, and which contained within its smoke-scented cavern the story of a life surmised—mine—before and after the crash of a relationship at a government guest house some aeons back.

The first thing I noticed when I took out the orange-black tin suitcase were the words 'For Sudipto' etched on the lid, the inscription having been made, in all probability, with a penknife. Opening the suitcase, I found it had been stuffed with dozens of my letters to Dadu, all inside their respective envelopes, some partly scorched and others almost intact, and a large diary. The diary had been damaged extensively, its plastic cover having melted and wrecked several pages at the beginning and at the end. The middle part however had a mixed fate. The part that contained my life, as grasped and committed to words in a fancy winding slant by a person who had long crossed the 'bar' to enter the luminescent corners of indelible memory. The part that featured a story, benign and sympathetic, but incomplete, in that it held no clue to the upheavals I would eventually append while being tormented by the relentless tick-tock of a jailer's clock.

Dadu's sketch of my character and predicament, reconstructed from the remains of the singed manuscript, appears next. The diary however stands restored to the Mukherjee family, since I had found it to contain, besides my limited biography, several entries devoted to the Chatterjees of Allahabad and other assorted characters whom I had no interest in knowing intimately. The tin suitcase with the inscription and the pages of the diary devoted to my story remain with me.

Fictional Non-fiction

Sudipto's Album

—*Dwarakanath Chatterjee*
Jhargram

I wonder if I can do it.

Sudipto Banerjee was a college lecturer. He taught English literature at Bengal Renaissance College on Surya Sen Street, off College Street, Calcutta. A reluctant academician, his first love had been badminton—goodminton, he would contradict—but a recurrent patellar dislocation and a morbid fear of surgery had dislodged his dream of picking up the mantle from Prakash Padukone. Sadly, the lecturer's contentious word play, besides his somewhat dated expertise in matters literary, had made him the subject of a nasty anagram: Stupido. But he never complained.

Sudipto lived near Ballygunge Phari in South Calcutta and, according to him, faced a Hamletian dilemma every working day. Each time he spied a red double-decker from afar while waiting at the bus shelter either at College Street or Ballygunge Phari, he would wonder if the approaching behemoth, a lumbering remnant of the Raj era perpetually on the verge of being phased out, was a '2B or not 2B'—2B being the bus that plied between his home and college. But again, the wisecrack did nothing to encourage Sudipto's uncharitable students to restore the correct sequence of letters in his name.

Tall and fair by Bengali standards, with long legs and a no-longer-slim waistline, Sudipto still cut a somewhat attractive figure. But it was none of these features that could be held liable for the fleeting second glance that Sudipto sometimes elicited from women for whom abundance of facial hair scored over muscular excess on the index of male attractiveness. His strength was his immense walrus moustache, his supposed inheritance from his great grandfather, a reputable supplier of stage props during the Girish Ghosh era of Bangla theatre.

The nickname Stupido eventually reached the ears of his wife and his school-going daughter. And while Sraboni seethed in anger and blamed her 'callous' husband for allowing the spiteful moniker to flourish for so long, little Titir urged her 'brave' father never to feel sad or cry when wicked people bullied him. '*Sticks and stones may break my bones, but words will never hurt me,*' she kept reciting to herself, in between stifled sobs, repeating her father's favourite lines from *How Green Was My Valley*.

'Why don't you do something about it?' Sraboni cried in desperation at the end of a long sermon on the virtue of being able to preserve one's dignity even in the most trying of circumstances, and then threatened to confront the principal of Bengal Renaissance College herself with her complaint.

'Oh no! Don't get so upset. After all they are kids, you know. And the more you complain about these things, the more they stick,' Sudipto counselled his infuriated wife. 'Besides, I have a feeling that in some ways the nickname is not entirely undeserved.'

The addendum set Sraboni on fire: 'There you are, Swami Sudiptananda! I knew it! And why do you deserve it, may I ask? For some stupid sins that you committed in a past life? When you were a jumping ape? Well, let me tell you this. I don't mind your students calling you Stupido, no, not at all. You can live happily with your past karma, but what about us? What about Titir? Why are you making a little child pay for your sins? As it is you hardly have any time for her. You know what, the least you could have done is to get a few of those rascals rusticated from college. That would have taught them and their hangers-on a lesson! But look at yourself. You know, you should have joined Bharat Sevashram or Ramakrishna Mission after Mrinalini discarded you, instead of getting your mother to con me into marriage. Oh why did I let you give up that software job! Why did I let you shift back to Calcutta when I knew your actual motive was to return to Mrinalini? To live in the hope of running into her every time you stepped out of the house? Oh, what did I do to deserve all this!'

Sudipto saw no point in continuing the conversation. He offered a wan smile to his fuming wife, patted his clearly distressed daughter, got up silently and locked himself in the study. The 10x8 feet cell with a small window to the west was actually a servant's room that the Banerjees had filled up with books and an ancient mahogany secretariat table, a family heirloom.

The table, complete with six drawers, a green rexine cover and a cracked glass top over it, had once belonged to Sudipto's great grandfather. And so had the three decorative paperweights resting on the thick-gauge glass sheet with their slightly concave base and rounded dome, displaying from within their confines flowers with tiny leaves, butterflies and a dancing couple. Family lore had it that Sudipto's great grandfather had originally procured four lead glass paperweights all the way from French factories for a king's ransom but that he had hurled one of them at his wife in a fit of rage only to see it overshoot the target, hit the wall and land on the table in shattered pieces, with one large piece fracturing the table top. Sudipto was happy that his genetic inheritance had not stretched beyond the thick walrus to include such traits as violent irritability.

Sudipto turned the key to the left bottommost drawer two-and-a-half times—the halal rite, he would have chuckled in less stressful times—and fishing out a thick spiral-bound photo album placed it on the table. A smile lit up his face.

For quite some time Sudipto did not open the album but kept staring at the fading cover, the implausible pattern of paisleys and roses giving up their respective colours of yellow and red to the universal reducing agent, time. The album was his life, partly in black-and-white and partly in colour. It was full of randomly stuck images that probably would not have meant much to most of the protagonists featured, but nevertheless recounted to him a story—a sort of fictional non-fiction of which he had been the witness.

Closing his eyes, Sudipto felt the long edge of the album with his right index finger. After a while, he let out a subdued 'yes' and opened the book and his eyes. He was right. It was exactly the page he had wanted to turn to. At the centre of it was the black-and-white photo of a youthful Sudipto beside the towering Ghosh Jethu who had his long greying hair brushed back and whose keen eyes seemed to peer through two thick tumbler bottoms, reincarnated as lenses. The backdrop was their company quarters, 3/15, Fifth Avenue, AG Housing Colony, Ranchi, lit up on one side by the soft glow of a melting winter sun and obscured on the other by irregular slanting shadows, of several large trees that had missed the frame.

It had been a landmark year. Sudipto, having obtained an MA in English from the Calcutta University, had been recovering at home in Ranchi allowing the familial and the familiar to soothe his jangled nerves, when he landed his first job at a New

Delhi-headquartered business fortnightly as a trainee sub-editor. His mother had wept in relief and his father had distributed sweets among colleagues at the Office of the Accountant General (Bihar), among whom there was Ghosh Jethu, the scholarly office master. A polymath, the Accountant General (AG) was senior to Sudipto's father in designation, age and professional accomplishments, but would not allow such 'incidental reality' stand in the way of his frequent visits to the Banerjees in the evenings after office. Karmic connection, he would say, as he settled down in the sofa to discuss religion and politics over frequent cups of tea with his junior colleague. The conversations had been lessons by themselves for an impressionable Sudipto. Setting aside his studies, he would remain riveted to the stool at the corner, marvelling at Ghosh Jethu's erudition, his wry sense of humour and his command over several languages, notably Bangla, English and Sanskrit.

When the appointment letter arrived by courier, Sudipto's mother rushed to the nearby post office that had a public telephone and called his father in office to convey the glad tidings. Banerjee senior was ecstatic and suggested that Sudipto visit Ghoshbabu in the evening with sweets. After all, it was largely because of AG sahib that Sudipto had turned out to be so good in the languages, especially English, and that is what would have enabled him to clear the written test and interview despite having been away from books for more than a year and somewhat unwell.

Dressed in freshly laundered clothes, Sudipto cycled to the AG's bungalow that evening, picking up half a kilo of rosogolla, Ghosh Jethu's favourite, on the way from Kanar Mishti, the local sweetmeat shop. The only difficulty was that he had to hold the earthen pot steady in one hand so that the syrup did not drip, and manoeuvre the cycle with the other, negotiating the narrow serpentine shortcut from the shop to the bungalow tucked away in a quiet corner of the housing colony.

Receiving Sudipto at the portico, Ghosh Jethu exulted: 'Come Bhombol, come! I knew you'd turn up. Congratulations to you! You have done us proud. You know I'd often wonder if it was not unwise to let you neglect your studies and station yourself at the drawing room while your father and I solved, through mere dialogue, all the momentous problems facing our country and our times. But your eagerness and your occasional comments would quite impress me. I knew you were learning much beyond your years and your syllabus. You saved me embarrassment once when you got through to Presidency College. And now it's the second time.'

Sudipto handed over the pot of rosogolla to the servant watering the flower beds, touched Ghosh Jethu's feet and told him he would be joining office at Delhi from the first of the following month. Ghosh Jethu embraced him and then blessed him for long, running his hand on the young man's head over and over again.

'Baba asked me to seek your blessings. And also your advice on how I should conduct myself at a media house,' Sudipto said as he struggled to restore his coiffure.

'I'm no Getafix,' Ghosh Jethu remarked, adding, 'But why do you bother? Your strengths are enormous. They will take you a long way. You are honest, considerate and even-tempered. Besides, you write well and can crack *The Statesman*'s cryptic crossword in no time! Just allow your merit to flow out; it will find its own direction.'

'But Jethu, to tell you the truth, although I'm happy, I'm a bit nervous too. And I've never been to Delhi,' Sudipto confessed.

'That's normal. It's your first job. And the place is new. Besides, you carry such a huge burden of expectations, your parents' and even your own.'

Sudipto had coffee—a coveted beverage that had not been able to break the monopoly of Darjeeling First Flush at home—with Ghosh Jethu at the portico that evening. They talked of various things and about various people, among them two of Sudipto's favourite sportsmen: Prakash Padukone and Björn Borg. Finally, when he got up to take his leave, Ghosh Jethu, rather unexpectedly, said he did have some advice to offer: 'One, you must read more, much more. Your reading is poor, I'm sorry to say. Language skills are just an enabling factor. It's like having a good road map at your disposal. But the map is not the journey. And, two, you lack the RH factor. It can be a very serious impediment. You must find a way to develop an RH.'

It was as if Sudipto had been struck by a sledgehammer. He had known all along his reading was not quite up to the mark, his healthy examination scores notwithstanding, but to be told that on the face! By none other a person than Jethu! And what timing! The weakness had to be pointed out when he had just won a job offer, beating over sixty candidates in the fray! His ears reddened and he wished he had not turned up at Ghosh Jethu's bungalow with a potful of rosogolla, which in any case had not been served to him.

'Your silence and the colour of your ears speak a lot, my son. Your pride has been hurt. Isn't that so, Bhombol?' Ghosh Jethu asked.

Sudipto would not lie. He put a lid somehow on the volcano within and said yes. At that, Ghosh Jethu got up from his chair and hugged him the second time.

'Damn honest!' he said, adding, 'As always! Keep it up, young man. And mind it, you just proved me right.'

'About what?' Sudipto asked, bewildered.

'My observation about the RH factor.'

'What RH factor? I always thought there's nothing wrong with my B+ve,' Sudipto wondered aloud.

'Not the Rhesus factor in blood grouping my boy, but the Rhinoceros Hide factor—although the B+ve is itself a message: be positive. You know, when you go out there into the world of wonders, teeming with people, some holy and others sinful, many a person inferior to you in talent but superior in ambition or position will want you out of the way. You must have a rhino hide to protect yourself. You must have the ability to flick off undeserved insults, criticism; the ability to turn a deaf ear to hostile words, snide remarks, if they are unwarranted. In short, you must have the ability to prevent people from getting under your skin.

'And yes, there's one more thing. Remember, there will always be disappointments in life. Never brood over them. Try always to live in the present. It is only the present that is real.'

Before Sudipto left, Ghosh Jethu went inside and coming out of the study handed him a maroon bejewelled fountain pen.

'My father gifted me this pen when I cleared the civil service and opted for audit and accounts over administration or police service. It would have gone to my progeny if I had chosen to commit the folly which even Socrates could not actually defend with his quip that there is no flipside to marriage. But since I didn't marry, the "heirloom" must be handed down to someone whom I would not have resented being my son. Take it and put it to good use.'

'I would not have resented being my son', the words drifted in from across the gulf of years to chime in Sudipto's ears, bringing a smile onto his face that now featured, besides the walrus, the tentative imprint of a few age lines. 'What should I care about some pranksters calling me Stupido!' he said aloud at length as he took out the pen from the top right drawer. He looked at it for a long time, watching the tiny diamonds on the clip throw bright little spots on the wall opposite as he turned the 'writing instrument' over and over again in his hand. Then, caressing the raised logo embossed on the top of the cap, he closed his eyes again.

The right index finger ran over the long edge of the photo album. After a while, Sudipto opened the book and his eyes. Wrong! This was not the page he had wanted to turn to.

~

The colour print at the top of the page was a group photo. Sudipto was there in the last row, a young man with a blooming walrus in his twenties, along with several people of both sexes posing for the year-end issue of *Business Review*, the business fortnightly. And there was Maha, C.P. Mahalingam, the editor, in his late forties, bang in the middle of the front row, balancing on his toes (to look taller) and offering to the camera his contemptuous look and a scanty Bulganin. Initially, Maha had taken Sudipto under his wings but suffered a change of heart a few issues down the line. That was after the trainee had made some corrections in the 'Letter from the Editor' section without the despot's prior approval. In the letter, Maha had committed several blunders: he had written 'alternate' instead of 'alternative', 'John Hopkins' instead of 'Johns Hopkins', and the worst of all, 'Indo-China' instead of 'Indo-Chinese' or 'Sino-Indian'. Sudipto had been asked to go through the camera copy and had marked the corrections in pen without first referring to Maha.

It was a wet August night. Well beyond twelve. The editor, recently married for the second time, had gone out for dinner at around nine and not returned to office since. He had left his jacket dangling from his chair and his dripping red fountain pen uncapped—indications that he might, though not necessarily, saunter in later. And the staff, especially the trainees, could not leave office until they were certain the Editor had.

Maha came back at around 12.45 or so, with his fat wife, a freelance journalist, in tow. The duo spent some time chatting in the Editor's plush cabin and then Maha pressed the bell. Hamid Bhai, the old peon on duty, who had on several occasions fallen off his stool dozing, jumped up and rushed to the master's lair. 'Call Sudipto!' the boss screamed and Sudipto sat up in his chair. He proceeded sheepishly to the Editor's cabin even as the three other trainees at the editorial desk prayed anxiously for him.

'Who the fuck do you think you are?' shouted Maha, the moment Sudipto pushed open the glass door, even as Maha's wife, nursing an old issue of the magazine in a corner chair, smiled from ear to ear.

'Sir, haaave I...' Sudipto stammered.

'Who the fuck gave you the authority to touch my copy?' Maha thundered again.

Sudipto kept standing at the door, his ears red to the roots and his eyes fixed on his feet. He did not know what to do or say. His chest was getting tighter and his legs were about to give away. He tried to catch hold of the chair in front and Maha erupted again.

'Get your ass out of here, you bloody moron!'

Sudipto somehow staggered out of the Editor's cabin and collapsed in the corridor. Hamid Bhai hurried, picked him up and brought him to the desk. Shrill laughter rang out from the boss's cocoon.

By the time Sudipto could leave office it was almost 4 am. He reached home an hour later, took a cold shower and sat at the second-hand plywood dining table to write to Ghosh Jethu. Initially, he thought he would describe in detail the insults he had been subjected to in office, leaving out only the expletives, but could not get himself to organise his thoughts. Besides, the expletives deleted, there was not much left to report. In the end, the letter was brief:

Respected Jethu,
I was badly abused at the workplace today. The RH refuses
to grow.
I have decided not to attend office for some time—at least till
I receive your advice.
Pronam,
Bhombol

The next day Sudipto called up Maha's secretary from a telephone booth in the neighbourhood and requested the kindly lady to inform the boss that he was indisposed and would possibly rejoin after a few days.

Three days later a telegram from Ghosh Jethu arrived:

Bhombol RH takes time. Dont lose heart. Rejoin immediately.
Blessings Jethu

Sudipto went to office the next day without having slept the night. And the moment he got in, Maha summoned the nervous trainee to his cabin.

'So the young man is sulking, is it?' Maha taunted Sudipto, but changed tack immediately. 'Is your illness serious?'

'No sir,' Sudipto replied and found Maha gawking at him, his lower jaw scraping the table.

'Then, four days? Men here have taken just a few hours off to get married. And women have delivered here in this very cabin! What kept you away for four full working days?'

'Sir, I had first thought of quitting.'

'Then what stopped you?'

'I changed my mind.'

'To do me a favour?'

'No sir, to do myself a favour.'

'How's that?'

'I want to see if I can survive all this.'

'We'll see that too! Now get your ass out of here and start working.'

Returning to his desk, Sudipto did his duties quietly, avoiding conversation, got up at the stroke of seven and walked out of office. Maha hit the roof. How dare a trainee go home with the Editor still working his ass off! The next day, Sudipto was abused again, and this time filthier words were used and in public. But the apprentice put up no protest. He heard the boss out, staring into the distance all the while, and returned to his desk to complete the day's work. The routine continued for several months, after which Sudipto wrote to Ghosh Jethu again.

Respected Jethu,
I am trying my best to develop RH. Do you think I should
seek an appointment with the proprietor, Mr C.K. Jaitley, and

request his help? Mr Jaitley has a reputation for fairness.
Pronam,
Bhombol

Ghosh Jethu's reply was longer this time.

My Son Bhombol,
Keep working on your hide. Meanwhile, let me relate to you
a story from the Ramakrishna Kathamrita:
During the reign of Akbar the Great, in a forest somewhere near
Delhi—maybe not very far from where you now reside—there
lived a fakir. Many sought out this old man in the woods to
obtain his blessings and intercession in matters both spiritual
and mundane. At some point in time it occurred to the fakir
that he should entertain his visitors with hospitality. 'But where
would the money come from?' he wondered, and then came up
with a solution as well: 'Let me ask Emperor Akbar. It is said
he is kind to holy men.'

When the fakir arrived at the Emperor's palace, Akbar was
saying his Namaz. So the fakir went into the prayer room and
took his seat in a corner. He heard Emperor Akbar pleading
repeatedly with Allah at the end of the Namaz, 'Oh Allah!
Grant me wealth, make me rich!'

The fakir rose at once and was about to make his way out
of the room when the Emperor, by gesture, asked him to be
seated again. His prayers over, Akbar asked the fakir, 'It was
on your own that you came and sat here. But why did you
want to leave before I had finished?' The fakir said, 'I better not
speak about that to you. May I take your leave now?' But the
Emperor would not let off the fakir so easily. He was insistent.
Finally, the fakir said, 'Many people visit my hut out there in

the forest, so I came here to ask for some money. Sometimes,
I feel like feeding some people, giving something to someone.'
Akbar was surprised. 'Then why were you leaving?' he asked.
The fakir replied, 'When I saw that you yourself are a beggar,
begging for wealth and riches, I thought, "Why should I beg
of a beggar? I had better beg of Allah."'
Blessings,
Jethu

Months rolled by when one day, out of the rare August blue, Sudipto received a call from a software company, Indus Software & Advisory Services. The HR manager, Sunil Jain, at the other end first introduced himself, then talked about the company he was proud to work for, and finally asked Sudipto if he would be interested in taking up an editorial job with them. It was a middle management position and the work would be 'very very exciting', although the hours could be long. The company was on the verge of coming out with several software products, something that even its much bigger rivals had failed to do despite their huge balance sheet size, and needed 'non-engineers' to develop the manuals and promotional literature.

'We are not into body shopping, unlike our big brothers, who, I'm sorry to say, have not been able to develop a single software product worth the name till date. All that they do is supply engineers to clients overseas and earn a cut on their dollar wages. The poor slogging engineers are cooped up four in a room in hired apartments and made to share a single bathroom and kitchen. But the moolah is where the products are. Creativity is where products are. One has to go up the value chain, you see,' the manager went overboard as he hard-sold the job offer over the phone.

It was all too overwhelming for Sudipto.

'But how did you get to know of me?' he managed to ask after remaining puzzled for some time.

'Oh don't bother about that! Our head-hunters are all over the place, digging out original thinkers from the most unlikely locations. Besides, we take recommendations from reputable people seriously,' the HR manager replied.

Sudipto said he was not sure if he was 'original or aboriginal' and would first want to meet Mr Jain in person, get to know more about his company and the role proposed and only then say yes or no.

'Suit yourself Mr Banerjee. We are in no great hurry. Can we meet today evening? At The Inn? It's just a short walk from your office. Actually, we can have dinner together, if that is fine with you. And I can arrange to have you dropped home.'

Somewhat uncharacteristically, Sudipto agreed. Maybe it was the thrilling appellation 'Mr Banerjee' that clinched the deal.

Eventually, Sudipto joined Indus as a Technical Editor on probation. The first few months were punishing. It was training, training and more training all the time. From nine in the morning till 6 in the evening, six days a week, a hapless Sudipto, placed in a herd of recruits, rushed from one training room to another, surviving one presentation only to be clobbered by the next. And at the end of what he would later recount as the 'haani (damage) moon period', during which many a conscript would have perished but for the steady supply of coffee, cookies and bottled mineral water, he had to clear a three-hour written test and was handed a certificate, which proclaimed to the world he was now a confirmed technical editor, the company's first.

The job however turned out to be nothing as exciting as the HR manager had made it out to be and the company was nowhere close to developing off-the-shelf software products. But that did not bother Sudipto much. 'What is the alternate?' he would ask himself, dipping into his previous boss's vocabulary with sinful delight. Meanwhile, a steady stream of software manuals kept flowing into the Technical Editor's Inbox with almost the same text: press F1 to do this, F2 to do that, and in the end Quit, Update, Exit. The money was however good and the perks still better. There was a cab service that picked him up from his rented home in the morning and dropped him back at the end of the day. The lunch was good, with dessert served every day. The medical insurance was large, and it was the company that paid the premium on behalf of employees. Further, after three years of service, there were a host of soft loans that employees could access, including loans for home, furniture and car.

~

Sudipto trudged on, continuing with his repetitive job without complaint, obtained a promotion, bought a used car and a new apartment in a not-so-fashionable area of Delhi, drafted Sraboni into his life and put on weight, growing a small paunch that had to be concealed beneath folds of baggy shirts. He also became friendly with the formidable Managing Director, Fakir Uttam Chand Karmakar, who, after having got over his deep-seated animus against journalists, not least because of their 'incorrigible habit of reducing everything to abbreviations and acronyms', had taken a liking to him and begun to trust the technical editor with company communication, advertisement material and miscellaneous high-profile work. (On his part, the technical editor never drew anyone's attention to the calamity the managing director would bring upon himself if he were ever to put his initials to documents, as the departmental heads did.)

On one occasion, when a book had to be brought out on Indus's unlikely evolution from being a regional manufacturer of chemical fertilisers to one producing software programs for clients both on- and off-shore, the MD made Sudipto the leader of the project. Spared the monotony of routine work, Sudipto put his heart and soul into the new project, codenamed Darwin, and the dramatic coffee table book that his team eventually produced caught the attention of the venerable proprietor, Dr D.N. Srivastava, a keen aesthete and a keener businessman. It also earned him an invitation for lunch from none other than the grand old man himself.

The lunch at a five-star, one that traced its history to colonial times, proved a pleasing affair, with endless courses and conversation. Dr Srivastava congratulated Sudipto (and his team), complimented him on his language and design skills, and said the creative person hidden within the technical editor had at last found an opportunity to come out into the open.

'We will need more of your expertise when we go public,' he said, his eyes smiling from behind the half moons of his bifocal lenses. 'Maybe it is Karmakar who should have told you this, but we are planning to get listed on the stock exchanges and will be making an initial public offer shortly. There's a lot of documentation involved. I would want you to get familiar with the merchant bankers and contribute to the issue prospectus. I will send a note to your MD and cc you in.'

The office memo came in the very next day. Sudipto felt greatly encouraged by the glowing terms in which his participation in Project Darwin had been acknowledged and his future contribution to the issue prospectus anticipated. He would have preserved the note for posterity, had the proprietor not committed, unwittingly, the impropriety of dropping the 'i' from 'Public' in the subject line, where he had actually intended to write 'Initial Public Offering' in bold typeface. 'The damn spellchecker!' the technical editor cursed his fate.

Sudipto made a good job of what was assigned to him, earning considerable praise from the senior management, including the pitiless Finance Director, Ajith Nambiar, a thin, bald man with hairy forearms who kept squeezing stress balls all the time, conjuring up various sadistic images involving almost everyone in office. Eventually, the company went public, but the occasion, ironically, also marked a turn in Sudipto's fortunes. Weighed down by the pressure of having to show growth in profits every quarter lest the share price on the bourses take a tumble, investments that could not fetch immediate monetary returns, like those in research and publications, were increasingly set aside, employee welfare schemes pruned, and several costs cut. In many ways and in many activities, quantity took over quality, even as the strategic decentralization of power for quicker market response spawned several clever but unwise satraps, many of whom were now engaged in avenging themselves against the 'darlings' of the pre-listing regime. 'A welfare state has turned into a farewell state,' Sudipto lamented, staring uncomfortably at the steadily climbing attrition rates that were now in the public domain.

~

One of the first casualties of the switch-over to the new dispensation was the editorial department, and with it Sudipto Banerjee,

Senior Technical Editor. His monthly pay did not diminish, but a lid had been placed on his prospects and he had been made ineligible for several perquisites, including profit sharing, deferred incentive, employee stock options, car loan, magazine allowance, office cabin and so on. It was now only a matter of a few years before even the currently junior-most employee in core services would overtake his salary and the gap between him and his peers in the engineering and consulting departments would begin to be measured in light years. Further, according to the grapevine, head-hunters had been engaged to pick up low-cost non-core staff from the poorly-paying manufacturing sector and the media. ('Maybe aboriginal thinkers this time,' Sudipto wondered.) It was the apprehension, the declining respectability among colleagues, the gloating of employees in core services over their newly acquired superiority, and the torment caused by the official label 'Support Service' that prompted Sudipto to write a long letter to Ghosh Jethu, telling him of his abrupt fall from grace.

The reply was however brief.

My Son Bhombol,
Count your blessings. Besides, in our journey towards self-realization, suffering is most often the faster horse.
Blessings,
Jethu

Sudipto was greatly embarrassed. After a few days, gathering himself, he wrote back to Ghosh Jethu saying the real cause of his suffering, he had to admit, was his inflated sense of self-importance. Surely, even greed had seeped in over the years, silently and in the garb of the commonplace. And to be honest, he actually did not need more money. He already had an apartment of his own in the country's capital, a well-fed family, a Korean car and a decent bank balance. And what was a designation but an empty boast, airy nothing!

Sudipto did not expect Ghosh Jethu to reply to this letter, but he did.

My Son Bhombol,

Your introspection impresses me. But I also hope it is not loser's logic that you impose upon yourself. It should not be the case that you grow so fond of your cage, you begin to despise your wings.

At one time you were overly impressed with the transparency of certain people in your company. You must have by now realized that greater the transparency, higher the capacity to deceive.

I do not however suggest that you run after money or creature comforts or perpetually seek out opportunities to get an ego massage. You get a kick out of all that no doubt, but in senses more than one!

Let me tell you a story from the Bhagavata:

At some place along the coast some fishermen were catching fish when a kite flew in and swooping over the catch carried one away. But no sooner had it picked up the fish than dozens of crows began to chase the kite, flying in from all directions, cawing all at the same time and creating a great nuisance. When the kite dived, the crows did the same, and when it went up, the crows followed. There was simply no escape from the cacophonous murder of crows. Eventually the kite got so confused that the fish fell from its beak. And immediately, the crows gave up their chase and flew towards the fish.

*Left alone, the kite sat on the branch of a tree and heaved
a sigh of relief. Finally at peace, it said to itself: No fish, no
worries.*
Blessings,
Jethu

Sudipto read the letter a number of times and put it in his
wallet. He would read the story of the kite often, especially
while at office, in between software manuals and letters of
commerce. It helped him keep the focus away from his steadily
diminishing status and his stagnating income and savour the
simpler pleasures of life. The senior technical editor would
never turn down or drag his feet on any assignment, but had
reined in his enthusiasm to push frontiers. And over time, he
had largely mastered the art of accepting the unpleasant, even
his right patellar handicap.

Rubbing his hand over his right knee, Sudipto now closed
his eyes and remained drawn inwards for some time. Coming
out of the darkness and of the several years that had passed by
since his days at Indus he turned to a new page in the album.

~

There, in the corner, stood Paranjoy his arm round Sudipto's
shoulder, and both out of focus. The venue: The entrance of
The Inn, the Kafkaesque eatery that had been witness to Sudipto's
metamorphosis from a budding journalist to a technical editor.
The occasion 'august', literally so. Paranjoy, the one-time college
mate, had suddenly sprung up in Sudipto's life a cloudless
morning on Independence Day in Delhi's central business district,
holding an inherited Yashica and capturing in black-and-white

the showpiece Georgian architecture of Lutyens's Delhi named after the Duke of Connaught. Bridging a hiatus of over a decade, Paranjoy initially marvelled at how well Sudipto had preserved his frame and maintained his walrus and then began to talk about his job as an assistant professor at a Calcutta college. He taught English literature, Anglo Saxon poetry and Chaucer to be precise, and it was 'not what the job gives me, but what it leaves me with' that excited him. Unravelling the mystery, he said it left him with enough time to tend to his garden, relive his childhood via his mischievous son, go on vacation twice a year (once with family and on the second occasion alone), build up his photography collection, and generally do whatever he desired, solving crosswords for instance.

Sudipto wished he too could be his own master. And return to Calcutta in the bargain.

'Why don't you try your luck at Bengal Renaissance College?' Paranjoy asked. 'Remember that private college at the junction of College Street and Surya Sen Street? Apparently they have been looking around for an English lecturer for quite some time now. You would fit the bill. They want a First Class in both BA and MA and there aren't many such candidates around. You get in there as a visiting lecturer, and while on the job obtain a PhD, and presto, you are on the regular pay scale! Think about it,' he suggested, and then added, 'But your salary will take a hit. That is, unless you take up private tuition.'

'Salary be damned!' Sudipto told himself, adding, for emphasis, 'No fish, no worries!' Soon thereafter, he sold off his apartment and his car and took the plunge, but only to jump from the frying pan to the fire. Getting into Bengal Renaissance College had been unexpectedly easy, but once into the job, he found himself hopelessly out of depth. With the syllabus having been updated twice since Sudipto had graduated, many of the textbooks had changed and much new light had been shed on subjects he had once been familiar with. While Sudipto's quick comprehension and his precision in writing had once allowed him to clear college and university examinations with relative ease, it was a totally different stage he had invited himself to perform on now. And he found himself rather unwilling, but again with no 'alternate'.

The visiting lecturer's vulnerability got exposed quite early. Into his third month at Bengal Renaissance College, Sudipto was asked one day to fill in for a regular professor who had been laid low by an attack of gout. It was a special class for the final-year English Honours students, and the subject was literary theory. Sudipto, unable to wriggle out of the assignment, walked into the classroom with uneasiness written all over his face. And the moment he had noted the attendance in the register, up went a hand.

'Sir, could we have your comments on the latest edition of the *Johns Hopkins Guide to Literary Thinking and Criticism*? Do you think literary theory and literary criticism are different animals?'

Sudipto was at sea. He remained baffled for some time and then gathering his wits around him, remarked, 'Johns Hopkins, that's right! Some media editors write John Hopkins, without the "s" after John, and the sub-editors let that pass. Well, what about the university? What is your question?'

The students smelt blood. Going for the kill, one frail bespectacled girl wobbled up and consulting some printed document fired, 'Sir, do you think the concepts of mimesis and catharsis are still relevant today? And I have one more question: How does, in your opinion, Bharat Muni's *Natya Shastra* fare against Aristotle's *Poetics*?'

A wave of snigger swept through the classroom as Sudipto failed miserably in trying to prevent his ears from going red. It was time for RH to be pressed into service again. Ghosh Jethu's observation that his reading was poor had just passed the test of time.

After a while when the students had had their fill, Sudipto said he was in no position to answer the questions as he had not prepared for the class. But if he were given a chance and some time, he would revert—'not "revert back", that's a tautology!'—with meaningful material.

'Free period,' someone from the back benches demanded and the lone call soon became a chorus. Sudipto had no choice but to leave the classroom and while he was on his way out, another voice, from around the same location, mocked 'revert back!' while still another called out, 'Stupido!'

The anagram stuck.

Sudipto closed his eyes and shut the album. He remained still for a long time, wondering if the students would still have heckled him had he inherited his great grandfather's intimidating personality in addition to the walrus.

~

Sudipto turned to the album again.

Stuck in the middle of the page that opened, the solus was not a photo but a picture postcard, featuring an image perhaps plagiarised from some famous canvas. The theme ostensibly was immersion of Goddess Saraswati, her clay idol that is. In the dimly lit representation, at the far end of a rippled expanse of red waters it was just the face of the Goddess and one of her hands raised in a gesture of benediction that were visible. They too would soon go under water, just as the rest of the idol had. A discarded garland of marigold and some flower petals and bael leaves lay strewn on the blurred foreground. The composition was striking. The pathos of the impending departure, the pervading gloom, the discarded flowers, the parting blessing—everything had come together to convey a sense of loss that was overwhelming.

Sudipto stared at the postcard for some time and struggled to hold back his tears. It was the only card Mrinalini had ever sent him during their over-three years of understated romance. At the end of which period, things took a bizarre turn and he found himself dumped.

It is quite likely destiny would have taken a different turn if Mrinalini had not all of a sudden decided to go to the Jawaharlal Nehru University in faraway Delhi to do her post-graduation. The atmosphere at her home had grown stifling. The perennial fight between her parents, their exaggerated regret that they could have separated long back had she not come in the way, and her father's continual advice that she aim for a career in law rather than in soppy literature became unbearable the moment a window of escape presented itself as a prestigious scholarship at JNU. Mrinalini had qualified for the scholarship on the strength of her brilliant BA result.

Mrinalini left Calcutta teary eyed, promising to return the moment Sudipto cleared his MA and found himself employment. Sudipto was the only one who came to see her off at the railway station, having walked all the eight-odd kilometres from Hindu Hostel, it being a day when all public transport vehicles had been taken off the roads to protest an increase in fuel prices. And as the Rajdhani pulled away, he ran alongside the glazed window of the air-conditioned coach, occasionally clutching his right knee, although unable to see through the reflection. The thought that his sweetheart watched him from inside was enough reward for him.

Initially, Mrinalini wrote to Sudipto several times a week, first telling him of how much she missed him and then about JNU's sylvan campus, with its stately trees and manicured lawns, scurrying squirrels, several woodpeckers and the chance peacock. The commentaries also included, in their coverage, her friendly roommates, one among whom was an anglicized Bengali who nevertheless told her multiplication tables in Bangla, the boys in her class—especially Bhanu Pratap Sinha—who sometimes smoked pot and drew rum from cola bottles at the university cafeteria, the colourful fairs at Pragati Maidan and the many attractions that the city, once the abode of the Pandavas, held for her. Sudipto, though slightly unsettled at discovering in Mrinalini traits he was not familiar with, kept his composure and replied to her letters promptly. But barely a few months since the transfer, the epistolary torrent flowing in from Delhi thinned to a trickle, and the tone of Mrinalini's letters changed. She now spoke of freedom, complete freedom, the need to break free from all shackles, and the imperative of standing on one's own feet and scripting one's own destiny. It took very little for a bond to turn into bondage, she had now come to realize.

Sudipto was alarmed. His letters to Mrinalini grew feverish, both in content and frequency, but went largely unanswered. Mrinalini would eventually write, sometimes after three weeks or four, but the letters contained nothing to assuage Sudipto's growing apprehensions. She would either talk of the trees and birds, or of Bhanu and other male friends, all of whom seemed modelled either after Omar Sharif or Gregory Peck, depending on whether they were valiantly romantic or romantically valiant.

The letters had not a word on whether Sudipto was missed or if returning to Calcutta still figured among Mrinalini's priorities.

Sudipto suffered silently for long, but one day unable to bear the pain of having to bottle up everything within himself, he confided in Sraboni, the tall girl in his MA class with laughing eyes, a celestial nose and long dark hair, the girl who seemed to be made of gold and the only one he had been close to. Initially, Sraboni offered only compassion. She never complained about Mrinalini hogging the conversation all the time. She comforted Sudipto saying he had to allow himself time to come out of heartbreak and that he could depend on her to stand by him through thick and thin.

From then on, every day after classes, Sudipto would take the minibus to Babughat with Sraboni, from where she would catch a ferry to cross to the other side of the Ganga where she lived. Sudipto would keep standing on the riverbank, indifferent to the jostling crowd, and watch the ferry chug away slowly into the distance until he could no longer make out which among the teeming dots on the deck was his saviour. It was only after the ferry had anchored at the other bank that he would return, boarding an overcrowded ordinary bus back to the hostel. It was a daily ritual, disrupted only on days the university remained closed. Little by little, Mrinalini receded from their conversation to yield place to everyday events, among them the sights and thoughts that occupied Sraboni on her 'lonesome' journey back home and during university holidays: the small waves of the Ganga reflecting the orange rays of the setting sun, the occasional leap of the river dolphin only to entertain, some class lecture that had simply been too good, a film that was worth another watch, some game that the Indian cricket team should have won but did not, an eventual piece of reality that had turned the tables on confident prediction. Sudipto's baffled monologues on the inscrutability of human nature were gradually replaced by Sraboni's enlightened accounts, and they held no complaint or remonstrance.

It was during the autumn break for the first year MA class that Sudipto told Sraboni, somewhat sheepishly, that he was perhaps falling for her and was not sure what he must do about it. Sraboni only smiled, tousled his hair and said, 'Carry on Jeeves!' It was just after they had come out of Metro Cinema on Chowringhee, having watched the Omar Sharif-starrer *Doctor Zhivago*.

Carry on Sudipto did, not without some discomfort, watching Sraboni gradually fill up the empty space that Mrinalini had left behind and weave her dreams about him. And if Sraboni's imaginings could be turned to reality, they would someday in the not-too-distant future have a small cottage at Kausani, where a school going Sraboni had once spent a summer week with her doting parents. The wooden cottage would be facing the majestic peaks of Nanda Devi, Trishul and Panchchuli, which a gainfully unemployed Sraboni would gaze at the whole day, watching them put on newer shades, from an unreal pink to blazing gold, as the sun travelled the azure of the overarching sky. Sudipto meanwhile would be running a small tourist taxi service, taking visitors here and there across the picturesque hill station that offered a panoramic view of the grand Himalayas.

The pattern of events broke all of a sudden one afternoon, just a few days before the MA finals. The unexpected letter from Mrinalini read: *Hi Sudipto, I'm back!!! Thought you'd know. In fact, I've been back for over a week now. See you at Flury's, 4.30 Saturday. Ha ha! M.M.*

Sudipto received the summons a mere twenty-two hours before the proposed rendezvous. He could not sleep that night.

He had not expected Mrinalini to return to Calcutta even in the distant future, but now that she had, he found himself besieged by several conflicting emotions. He had been deeply hurt, but found himself rather happy, in fact quite happy, at Mrinalini's return; he was eager to see her, but a sense of foreboding filled him; he was the injured party, but had perhaps used that status to his advantage.

Sudipto wished, if only for a moment, that he could confide in Ghosh Jethu. But then, he was not sure a bachelor would understand. Besides, the conflict was not one that could be resolved with reason. And what was reason but a mere pleader, a bonded advocate, for the heart? It merely did the heart's bidding. And if the heart was corrupt, so would reason be. The truth was that his heart was corrupt, greedy, insecure. And with such a crooked heart for its client, what would the poor advocate do but obfuscate! The right course of action could emerge only if he could unravel the default settings of his heart. That would help him reach a decision. But wait, even if he could figure out the settings and neutralize them, how would that help? Without the settings, where would desire be? Nonsense! And wasn't he straying, the chronically confused person that he was? Wasn't he getting farther and farther away from the job at hand? The job being to prepare himself for the meeting with Mrinalini at Flury's the coming afternoon?

Sudipto got out of bed the moment he heard the crows. The brushing and washing over, he sat with his books, turning pages mechanically and reading whatever appeared before him. Sometime later, the ward boy at Hindu Hostel brought him breakfast, which he had at the study table, then continued with his robotic reading, had lunch sometime later and finally got dressed and left for Flury's.

By the time Sudipto landed at the upmarket café in Park Street, Mrinalini was already seated at a corner table, sipping coffee. How much she had changed! Slightly plump, wearing stylish clothes and with her sunglasses still on her, she looked a woman in complete command. Mrinalini got up the moment she saw Sudipto, who marvelling at her sudden gain of height, could offer only a limp hand to shake.

'Hey, you look spaced out. What's wrong?' Mrinalini asked, an eyebrow raised.

'Well, do I? But you look gorgeous. And so much taller!'

'Heels stupid, I'm wearing heels. You didn't expect me to grow at this age, did you?' Mrinalini laughed, just as she would have in the olden days before JNU.

'But sir, there's good news,' she leaned forward excitedly as Sudipto stiffened. 'I've been selected by the Wanderlust Group of Luxury Hotels at a campus recruitment drive, and guess what, I'll be working for them here in Calcutta from now on! What do you say to that, hey?' she grinned.

'But your MA? Have you got your results already?'

'Oh you've remained the same!' she leaned back. 'When someone says she's just got her first job, courtesy demands you first congratulate her and maybe ask for a treat. Only after that you discharge your stupid questions. Oh when will you learn Sudipto, when? And, by the way, I managed a First Class second in MA too. Hah! Exams and results happen on time at JNU unlike your Calcutta University. Your MA session is running late by, how many, four months now?'

Sudipto was embarrassed. 'Congratulations, certainly! Both for the result and the job.' Then collecting himself he added, almost as an afterthought, 'The treat will be my pleasure of course.'

Silence fell between the one-time lovers, both not knowing how to fill the vacuum that the separation of two years had created between them. Mrinalini kept drumming her fingers on the table while Sudipto stared at his own hands. At length Mrinalini made an attempt: 'You haven't asked me how I'm doing, or how I've been. You're not complaining that I did not answer some of your letters. Don't you think that's somewhat unusual?'

Sudipto kept silent for long, weighing this phrase and that in his mind. 'I thought you had lost interest in me Mrinalini. I did not want to pester...' he said eventually.

'Oh no, it's not that way at all,' Mrinalini cut in by instinct, and then made a somewhat unconvincing attempt at elaborating. 'You know, when I tasted freedom for the first time, I did not want anything to come in the way. I would not barter it away for anything. And by anything, I mean anything. In fact, you know, when freedom first came my way, I went berserk, even wayward you could say. Compensatory behaviour, I guess. I had to make quite an effort to get my act together and focus back on studies. And when that happened, again I would stand no distraction.'

'I seek no explanation, I have never sought...' Sudipto wanted to say, but Mrinalini resumed, now almost in a whisper, 'I know I treated you badly, Sudipto, very badly indeed. I'm sorry for that. It is to offer my sincere apologies that I called you here.'

Sudipto kept staring at the table. He was not sure he would be able to keep a lid for long on the tumult rising within. The waiter intervened and Mrinalini ordered sandwiches for her yet-to-be-employed guest and coffee for both.

'Won't you say something?' Mrinalini asked after a while, when the waiter had served the order and taken away the empty cup. But Sudipto sat still, his eyes downcast, shoulders slumped.

She stirred her coffee briskly, apprehensive that the meeting was heading for a disaster.

'And what does freedom mean for you now?' Sudipto barely managed to get the words out after what seemed like ages. He could not trust himself to meet her gaze.

Mrinalini collected herself quickly. 'Sudipto, to come straight to the point, I don't think we should get married. We had a great time together. In fact, without you, Dadu and Jhargram, I wouldn't have been able to cope with the pressure building up at home. But for me, the past is too precious to be spoilt by everyday bickering. I have done you grave injustice. I have broken your heart. It's not something you'll get over in a hurry. But if we were to get married, this phase of my life, with all your hurt and anger, will come up every other day. It is bound to. I have seen that in my family, with my parents. I think it is in the interest of both of us to look upon our affair as a closed chapter. A chapter that may be read over and over again, with a twinge in the heart each time, but never brought to life and spoilt by pettiness.'

It appeared she had planned the little speech well beforehand, but Sudipto made no comment. After some time, still staring at the table, he asked the only question that mattered now.

'And what are your plans, if I may know?'

Mrinalini did not hesitate a second. 'Nothing definite... All I can say at this moment is I will do everything to be financially independent.'

She paused for a moment, and in a different voice, continued somewhat hesitantly. 'I do not think I will have the kind of romance I had with you ever again. There will probably never be anyone with whom I will be able to open up the way I have with you... Maybe as the years go by I will marry some decent chap, to settle down, have a home, have some routine, security. You see, and I've come to realize this, it is still difficult for a woman to manage on her own even in this day and age.'

Sudipto did not look up. He could feel the ground sinking beneath him and as his anxiety rose, he held on to the table, desperate not to break down, not to make a show of his misery in public. It took him long to find his voice.

'What wrong did I do to you Mrinalini?' he almost choked.

'Oh no my friend, you have done me no wrong. Honestly, none. It is only that I have changed. And this changed person no longer deserves you the way she did earlier... Be happy, Sudipto, and forgive me if you can...'

Mrinalini got up, called the waiter, stuffed some currency notes in his hand and left.

Devastated, Sudipto remained seated at the table, watching through the mist in his eyes a thin layer of cream appear on the surface of the untouched coffee as it turned cold. It was only when the waiter came and asked him if he was feeling all right, that he could pull himself together, get up from the chair and walk out of the café. He wandered aimlessly on Park Street for some time and finally turned up at the bus stop. There he bumped into Mrinalini again. She too was waiting for her bus, standing in front of a tattered cinema poster of *Doctor Zhivago* and holding a large gift-wrapped box.

'We've got a second telephone at the hostel recently. Would you want the number?' Sudipto burst forth, his sweating face contorted in an odd smile. 'And can I call you at office sometimes, if you are allowed to take personal calls that is?'

If Mrinalini was alarmed, she did not show it.

'Sure! And yes, my folks have got me a phone in my room too. It's better you call me at home. I'm staying at our Shyambazar house, at least for the present. Let's see how things pan out now that I'm no longer a dependant.'

She asked Sudipto to hold the gift-wrapped box, took out a piece of paper and pen from her handbag and gave him her new number.

Sudipto stared vacantly at the chit in his hand, the odd smile still pasted on his face, until the bus for Shyambazar arrived. It would go via College Street, Sudipto's stop. Mrinalini helped her one-time beau board the bus, and waved him off saying she had some appointment somewhere else.

Back at the hostel, Sudipto locked himself in his single room and collapsed. He could not hold himself back any longer and breaking into sobs, wept inconsolably. Oh, how would he live without Mrinalini? How could he live knowing that she had married someone else, was living with another man? And that she was here in this very city raising someone else's kids? How could all those years, those dreams, be burnt to ash, buried and forgotten? How would he live with so much pain, ceaseless pain? What was there left in life worth living? What solace could Sraboni ever bring to him now that grief had eaten away his heart? And yes, Sraboni! What about her? What would he tell her? To go on loving him even as he continued yearning for someone else? Or that she should now erase him from her mind, pack up and go her own way? Just because Mrinalini had returned? What crime had the poor girl committed? Was this the way one repaid someone for pulling him back from the edge of the precipice? Someone who had offered him a shoulder to weep on?

Late into the night, when the tears had dried, Sudipto got up, staggered through the dark corridor to reach the hostel clinic at the corner, hesitated for a moment and then broke the window pane with his fist. Putting his bleeding hand through the jagged hole he groped for the bolt, found it, and threw the window open. Climbing into the room, he switched on the lights and began rummaging the drawers and cupboards. The frantic search yielded entire strips of sleeping pills. He swallowed them, an entire fistful, all at one go.

But he survived.

When Sudipto opened his eyes, he found three faces gazing intently at him as he lay on an unfamiliar bed. While his father's face showed utter befuddlement, his mother was on the brink of tears. It was only Ghosh Jethu who seemed to offer a smile, his trademark smile.

'Welcome back,' Ghosh Jethu said, 'how was it upstairs?'

Sudipto stared at him for long and grew nervous as he came out of his stupor.

'Where have you brought me? What place is this?' he asked anxiously. Ghosh Jethu ran his hand on Sudipto's head and told him he was in the safest of places, a hospital. The shift had been necessary because of the events since the previous evening. An ill-considered attempt had been made at escaping the consequences of the choices one had made. But providence had intervened, prompting the unsuccessful escapist to live with those very consequences like a man. Sudipto pressed his shaking hands, the right one in a heavy bandage, against his ears as tears ran down his cheeks. A doctor came in, smiled at Ghosh Jethu, said something about having once attended the bureaucrat's lecture on 'Money and the Spiritual Warrior' at Calcutta Club, and issued an almost illegible discharge certificate.

Emerging from the hospital, Sudipto got into a car, which took them straight to the AG Bengal guest house where his parents and Ghosh Jethu had put up after flying in from Ranchi. He took a few days to come out of the daze and appeared for the MA examinations at his father's insistence.

When the last paper was over, Sudipto walked up to Sraboni and taking her into an empty classroom told her, 'I'm extremely sorry to be saying this, but I don't think we should carry on. I don't think we should ever get married...'

And before the shocked girl could say anything, Sudipto made to walk away. Pausing some way down the corridor, he looked back, returned to a still-stupefied Sraboni staring blankly at the blackboard and poured out a postscript almost in a single breath:

'I will always remain grateful for the way you got me out of the mess. In fact, without you I wouldn't have been alive perhaps. But we can't carry on. It won't be good for either you or me. Let's stop it... Sraboni, you deserve a much better person than I have ever been or can be... God bless you.'

With that he rushed out, got into Ghosh Jethu's office car waiting at the main gate and returned to the guest house. Promising to himself on the way that he would not dwell on the subject ever again.

Sraboni tried visiting Sudipto at the hostel only to be told that he had been whisked away by his parents and was now staying at the AG Bengal guest house in Kidderpore, and that no visitors were allowed there. Frantic, she tried calling Sudipto a number of times at the guest house, but every time it was his mother who took the call and told the pleading girl that her son was not well, was undergoing counselling, and it was best he did not speak to or meet anyone outside the immediate family.

After some time the calls ceased.

Then, all of a sudden one evening, in walked Mrinalini seeking an audience with Sudipto. The senior Banerjee sent his wife to negotiate with the unwelcome visitor waiting at the reception, but the mother failed in her assignment.

'What makes you think I'll do him harm, Auntie?' Mrinalini demanded, brushing aside the nervous mother's misgivings. And folding her arms across her chest asserted, 'And sorry to say this Auntie, but I don't think you know your son as well as I do. If you don't let me in, the regret will be yours. I can't be standing here in a guest house for eternity. Besides, do you think you can prevent Sudipto from doing in future what I'm told he tried to do just a few days back? I think, for the sake of your own son's welfare, you should let me in. But it's your wish. You decide.'

Marching into Sudipto's room, Mrinalini banged the door shut and fired straight at her one-time beau. 'What made you do that, you fool?' she demanded, her voice shaking.

Sudipto told her the entire story, including the part about him and Sraboni.

Mrinalini remained silent for a long time, stroking her chin and chewing her lip. Eventually, making up her mind, she said, 'But given the baggage, both mine and yours, I think it's all the more sensible that we don't marry each other.'

At this point Sudipto began pleading with Mrinalini.

'Please, let us give it a try. For my sake, for old time's sake. If it doesn't work out eventually, as you mistakenly think, you can always walk out. You already have a job, a good income, you are financially independent. And as for the baggage, I promise you here and now I will never hold your JNU days against you. I'll never raise the topic, I swear upon my life, upon anything you want me to. And if I ever do, you will be free to leave me that very instant.'

Mrinalini did not speak for long, her face turned away towards the wall on her right. Then she sat up in her chair and looking into Sudipto's eyes said she had made up her mind to marry someone in her office; this gentleman had proposed to her sometime back and she had given him her consent recently.

Sudipto was stunned. His mouth open, he kept staring at Mrinalini, unable to think or utter a word. A long time later he brought himself to ask, 'Are you in love with him?'

'I don't know... Sudipto, the line between friendship and love is a fine one indeed. I don't know how to answer you. All I can say is he's the happy-go-lucky sort; your troubles simply turn insignificant in his company. And he's very open and accepting, someone who will not hold my past against me, someone who will not hate my friends, especially you... Someone who accepts me for what I am. And he's such a good painter, I can't tell you!' She forgot herself and smiled.

'Does he know about us?' Sudipto asked, clutching vainly at a straw of hope.

'Yes and no. He knows you are the best friend I've ever had. Perhaps he guesses there's been something between us...'

'Oh, can you please give me his number?' Sudipto's voice was desperate, beseeching. 'Let me tell him about all that has happened between us, about how much you mean to me. Let me plead with him to let you off. Let me try at least once. Let me...'

'You'll do nothing of that sort,' Mrinalini cut in, ice in her tone. 'Oh I can't imagine you saying all this!'

It seemed she would storm out of the room, but after a moment's hesitation settled back in her chair. Silence took over as both fought their own lonely battles within, one to raise from the dead his old romance, the other to have a new one. Finally, Mrinalini let out a sigh and got up to leave.

'Perhaps our paths will cross again. And till such time, I wish you the best in life. Be happy, Sudipto.'

~

The tap-tap of determined heels on the hard mosaic floor still echoed in Sudipto's ears from across the chasm of decades. Hours had passed since he had shut himself in the study, refusing to get into an argument with Sraboni over how he should deal with certain discourteous students in his college. The setting sun now peeped in through the small window, filling the small room with an orange glow and resurrecting from the hollows and dells of memory small wind-spurred waves on the Ganga that a lonesome girl had at one time reflected on.

That girl was now his wife, the star-crossed girl who had been persuaded into tying the knot with him as much by the still-glowing embers of an unfinished romance as by his pleading mother's assurance that her son's neurotic dependence on Mrinalini would simply melt away in the warmth of connubial bliss—a bliss that Sraboni alone could offer.

But what had Sraboni got out of all these years with him? Had he not let her down? Had he not failed in dissuading himself from peering wistfully ever so often through the tremulous prism of memory to watch with bated breath the play of light and shade beneath the swaying foliage of the sal, mahogany and neem at Jhargram, or the flickering shapes on the lime-washed walls of Dadu's bungalow lit up by a fitful lantern on a long winter night, and find all these gather for him the smiles and fleeting looks, the whispers and fragrant touch that Mrinalini had once given so freely of?

And had he not failed—his best intentions be damned—to turn himself into Sraboni's sheltering rain tree that even the scorching summer sun could not stop from blossoming? Had he not failed in building for her with the vines and twigs of fancy, a small hilltop nest staring incredulously at the imposing Himalayas, the majestic peaks of Trishul, Nanda Devi, Panchchuli?

Caught in the crosscurrent and watching his small boat of sanity whirl maddeningly, unable to deal with the spiral pull that would soon take it down to dark gasping depths, Sudipto held on to the edge of the secretariat table with both hands and closed his eyes. But there was no respite. Now, on the dark inner screen emerged the picture postcard Mrinalini had once sent him: the image of Goddess Saraswati drowning slowly across a rippled expanse of red waters, with a hand raised in a gesture of benediction—a parting blessing. The kindness was stifling, as was the prospect of a slow, painful death.

'No!' Sudipto cried out and opening his eyes slammed the album shut. He remained slumped in his chair for some time, then got off and sat on the floor facing the wall. Closing his eyes he gradually lost himself in prayer, asking for neither riches nor fame, love nor peace, but only stillness—the strength to bear his cross.

~

The Banerjee household had been silent for long. Since the time Sudipto had locked himself in the study, seeking the solace of his photo album. There had been no lunch. Little Titir had been handed a hastily prepared sandwich by her mother and told to keep herself busy with her books and games. She had amused herself for some time and then all noise had ceased.

The doorbell rang. Once, twice, three times. Jerking Sudipto out of his prayer and sending him rushing to the front door. The door was ajar and across the threshold stood a bald man with no eyebrows and no hair on his cheeks or chin holding a parcel. It was a small packet Ghosh Jethu had couriered from

Siliguri, the gateway city in North Bengal where the retired AG had stationed himself at a needy relative's for the past several weeks. Sudipto stared at the packet for long and gradually a smile spread beneath the walrus. 'Principle of synchronicity, or meaningful coincidence,' he muttered under his breath as he cut through the scotch tape and thermocol packing to take out triumphantly a pair of gold-rimmed sunglasses in a leather case, besides a small note.

My Son Bhombol,
I strayed into Hong Kong market last evening and picked up the sunglasses for you. The parcel should reach you well in time for your coming birthday. The model will go well with your walrus, methinks, and should help you cut out the glare of the past as you look ahead. The past, they say, is destiny; the future, free will.
Love,
Jethu

P.S. The ad line for the sunglasses says the product is 'Genuine since 1937'. Never imagined a business enterprise would so openly admit it sold fakes earlier!

'Typical Ghosh Jethu,' Sudipto could not help laughing as he read the postscript. He put on the sunglasses and beginning to feel uplifted looked around for his wife and daughter, expecting compliments. But neither of them was there; both, he assumed, were fast asleep, with the little one perhaps curled up beside the mother on the nuptial bed. Still wearing the sunglasses, Sudipto shuffled around in the dark for some time, rather pleased with himself and his approaching birthday, and went into the kitchen to make coffee and drinking chocolate. The beverages ready, he now sought to surprise his family with hotel-style room service, and entered the bedroom with large steaming mugs and a plate of assorted biscuits balanced on a wood-and-cane tray that Sraboni had kept aside for serving guests.

'Coffee for the lady and drinking chocolate for the little one,' he announced dramatically, placing the tray on the bedside table and switching on the lights.

There was no one.

Taking off the sunglasses, Sudipto went to the smaller bedroom, looked up the two wash rooms, but there was no one anywhere. It took quite a while for reality to sink in. And even if it had not, there lay an open letter on the dining table placed beneath a bowl of apples, one partly bitten off perhaps by Titir.

Sudipto,
Enough is enough. You can keep yourself locked in the study for ever and stare at Mrinalini's photos all your life. I'm leaving with Titir. For good. I mean it.
Do not create a scene at my parents' home by visiting us there. They are respectable people. And do not ever send money or gifts to any of us.
Wish I had never met you!
Sraboni

Sudipto read and reread the letter many times over, with tears streaming down his cheeks, before collapsing on the bed, clasping Titir's little pillow to his chest. He stayed like that for a long time and when it was dawn staggered into the study to write to Sraboni.

Dear Sraboni,

I accept your charge. Yes, I've not been able to get over Mrinalini (although it was not her photos I was looking at). And I can understand how you must feel about it.

Sraboni, I have always held you deserve a much better person than I've ever been or can be. So go ahead if you have anyone in mind.

I don't know how I will apologise to poor little Titir, if and when I get to meet her in this life.

God be with the two of you.

Sudipto

~

I started by saying, a la Maugham in '*Salvatore*', that I wondered if I could do it and now I must tell you what it is I have tried to do. I wanted to see if I could hold your attention for a few pages while I drew for you, taking the recourse of a photo album, the portrait of an ordinary man, a simple college lecturer, who perhaps did not have the Italian fisherman's native goodness to recommend him, but possessed a quality that too is rare: civility, plain civility.

An Affidavit

I wish Dadu's sketch of my character and halfway predicament—drawn obviously from the copious letters I routinely wrote him and from his own hypotheses—could be abridged and inscribed on my cenotaph in gothic minuscule. Yes, gothic minuscule, because the script, as Renaissance Humanists believed, is a barbaric one, appropriate, in the context of modern times, for the portrayal of a crafty barbarian let through into enlightened society by the noble-minded, the innocent—the seraphs, who cannot tell between the sly and the civil.

And this epitaph—if I have my way from beyond the Labyrinth—would also include, in the same gothic font and point size, my take on Dadu's account.

In a postscript?

No, I would rather have an affidavit, however inappropriate that be on a wishful memorial plaque. An affidavit to tell the tombstone tourist that Dadu's Sudipto is both me and not me. His Sudipto is perhaps what I should have been; maybe would have been, had a different collage been attempted from the same frayed pieces of my blighted life.

I believe Dadu, while writing about me, had been taken in by the leaves, the flowers, and the deluding fruit. Forgetting, in the excitement of his discovery, that there must reside beneath the innocuous surface of the ordinary soil, and curled up in the unseen rhizome, tendencies and instincts that cannot always be deciphered from such overground exhibits as foliage and blossoms. Thus, Dadu's Sudipto, besides being incomplete, is misleading. The complete Sudipto must emerge only when the last word of this unforced confession has been written.

Stop!

Yes, I cannot argue the case any further. For that would take me ahead of my story by several events, which I cannot skip, given their burden of unanticipated separations and disquieting reunions.

Forsaken

It must have been a year since the fire at Jhargram and the Phoenix-like emergence of a singed tin suitcase from the smouldering debris that Dadu's forest bungalow had been reduced to. An unknown man, clad in the traditional Bengali attire of dhoti-kurta and with a smiling face, turned up at my apartment one Saturday afternoon and handed me an envelope. It was from Ghosh Jethu, whom I had not met or heard from in ages.

The letter was brief.

My Son Bhombol,
I have put up at my ancestral home at Barrackpore.
Please make it convenient to drop by the coming Saturday evening.
Keep well.
Love,
The Ghosh Who Walks

P.S. You will find my address at the bottom left corner of the envelope. From Barrackpore station take a rickshaw to Ghosh Bari. The fare is Rs 5.

It seemed as if the paroxysmal attacks that had come to periodically rack my solitary life would now cease and some semblance of order would be restored. Ghosh Jethu had left Ranchi soon after his retirement from service, having got his belongings packed and moved to the Barrackpore house. Thereafter, he had stationed himself at a relative's place in Siliguri, from where he would write once in a while and occasionally send gifts, the latest being the sunglasses, 'Genuine since 1937'. The last letter I had received from Ghosh Jethu, again from Siliguri, was the one in which he had expressed dismay at Sraboni's walking out on me and the hope that I would eventually emerge stronger from the ordeal, given that 'in our journey towards self-realization, suffering is most often the faster horse'—his favourite turn of phrase in the face of adversity. After that Ghosh Jethu had simply stopped writing and the letters I sent him came back with the confounding message 'Addressee Not Found'. I had been quite miffed at the disappearing act, perhaps more so because that was the time I had needed him the most. But I was happy at the out-of-the-blue summons from Barrackpore, the past peeve notwithstanding.

I took the Barrackpore Local, a fast train, from Sealdah station, not very far from Ballygunge Phari (where I lived, alone) the following Saturday evening and within less than half an hour was at Barrackpore, a river town that was once a major military cantonment and also the stage for several acts of rebellion against British rule during the nineteenth century. A typical suburban railway station, teeming with jostling people, nagging beggars and huckstering vendors, the railway station offered no clue to Barrackpore's historical moorings.

The ride on a rickshaw through a winding potholed road was mercifully brief and I soon stood before a massive red-brick house that appeared to have borrowed both its architecture and vintage from Government Eden Hindu Hostel—my home for five long years during college and university.

The intricately-carved front door with polished brass knobs was opened by the man who had delivered Ghosh Jethu's invitation at my apartment. He offered a namashkar with a warm smile, and guiding me to the wooden stairs indicated that my host was to be found on the terrace.

Stepping onto the rooftop, I was first greeted by a large round moon peering over an abundance of shimmering foliage that conferred upon the two-storey house a sort of botanical seclusion. And in that silvery light I spotted Ghosh Jethu seated in an easy-chair at the far end, his left hand resting on the adjacent table, his right on an open book on his lap, and his face turned westward, perhaps in the direction of the Ganga. Another easy-chair, awaiting occupancy, lounged on the other side of the tea table.

Ghosh Jethu turned towards me as he heard my footsteps and got up immediately. Keeping the open book on the table, he came forward and took me in his embrace.

'Bhombol, you look so much older! What happened?' he asked me with concern as I touched his feet and straightened up.

'It's the moon,' I smiled, not wanting to embark on a narration of my travails. 'And you look different too—younger, if you will permit me to say that!'

Ghosh Jethu laughed as he sat down. 'OK, I will not ask you about your troubles. In fact, the more you talk of troubles, the deeper they embed themselves in the mind. Troubles may come and troubles may go, but you should go on forever,' he patted my back.

A soft breeze, carrying the enchanting Lady of the Night on its unseen wings, blew gently across and the pages of the open book fluttered.

'What have you been reading, Jethu?' I asked, unable to make out the title of the book from the header.

'*The Sayings of the Buddha*. Are you familiar with The Enlightened One?'

'Not much,' I confessed, remembering he had once asked me to brush up on my reading.

'Imagine a night like this, a full moon night, several centuries ago,' Ghosh Jethu began in a soft meditative tone. 'And Ajatshatru, the king of Magadh, sitting on the terrace of his palace, unable to deal with his inner torment. Encouraged by the monk Devdatta, Ajatshatru has usurped the throne of Magadh, killing Bimbisara, his father, but is now unable to appease his conscience. The royal physician, Jivak, wants the suffering king to meet the Buddha. Initially Ajatshatru hesitates, but finally agrees. The Buddha and the king meet at Jivak's mango grove. But Ajatshatru is not one to surrender himself to a monk easily. Even in his torment, he makes his demand clear. What would he have to gain from a life of spirituality here and now—in this very life? The king has no patience for rewards after death. The Buddha smiles and the discourse begins.'

'What did the Buddha say?' I asked after waiting for him to continue.

'I suggest you read that yourself at your leisure. But what a dramatic setting for a sutra! And the conclusion is striking too. When Ajatshatru has left after the visit, the Buddha tells his monks that the king is truly ruined. If he had not taken the life of his father, he would have been blessed with a vision of the Truth even as he sat there listening to the discourse.'

We remained silent, the atmosphere introspective, watching the dazzling moon cast shadows on the open terrace. Eventually, Ghosh Jethu, following his own stream of thought, spoke out.

'In a way most of us are like Ajatshatru, minus the burden

of murder of course. We are impatient. We want deliverance here and now. And the good news is, deliverance is possible.'

'Deliverance from what?' I blurted out.

'From *dukkha*, suffering,' he smiled. 'You see, many are the forms suffering takes. Injuries—your recurrent patellar dislocation, for instance—cause suffering, and so does sickness. Then the suffering of having to part with what we want to retain; or the suffering of having something we want to avoid thrust upon us. Further, the suffering of coming to the realization that the things we wanted and got do not give us the contentment we thought they would. So, there is suffering from pain, from change, and from the conditioned nature of things.'

'But Jethu, isn't suffering inevitable? And how much of our own lives do we control anyway?' I sighed.

'Well, let us say we can't control the external environment in our ordinary state of being. But it always takes two hands to clap. What if we can control the other hand? That is, what if we can control our reaction to what is beyond our control?'

'I don't quite get you.'

'Look at the moon. It will be there even if you were to turn your eyes away from it, isn't it so, Bhombol? But...'

'Yes, but that is the point! Even if you were to turn your eyes away and pretend there is no moon, it would still be there!'

'Correct, but it would cease to affect you. And that is what you want!'

'Well, with the moon maybe you are right. But, say, I put my hand in fire and turn my eyes away, pretending there is no fire. Will the pain go away?'

'Ordinarily no, because your mind will continue to dwell on your hand, on the suffering, but in particular states of consciousness, yes—states in which you cease to identify yourself with your body and mind.'

But I would not take that.

'Jethu, you will admit that even if we accept such a state of consciousness is possible, it's not in the lot of ordinary men to ever reach that. For most people, Sudipto Banerjee included, that is fiction, fantasy.'

'Do you know Gandhiji had his appendectomy done without anaesthesia—while he continued to chat cheerfully with his disciples?'

'Yes, I have read about it.'

'You know how that was possible? Because he could detach his mind from the senses at will.'

'But how does one do that, Jethu?'

'There are ways, Bhombol. As Acharya Rajneesh has said, the question *how* is the right question; *how* requires a method, a technique, for resolution. *Why*, on the contrary, seeks an explanation. *Why* is intellectual, *how* experiential.

'The problem is, we confuse the intellectual with the experiential, philosophy with spiritual methods. Philosophy strives to answer the question *why the suffering*, in the process tying itself up in knots; spiritual methods on the other hand tell you *how to overcome suffering*.

'To understand *why*, all you require is an intellect. It is easy; if you understand language, you understand philosophy. Of course, it's another matter whether the explanation satisfies you. If you are satisfied, you accept the explanation and may even want to impose it on others—a recipe for strife, historically. And if you are not satisfied, either you go on with your search for the right explanation, or simply give up, believing the search is futile, a waste of time.

'But with spiritual methods, things are different. No belief is required. No explanation is sought. The method simply says, "try this technique and you will know".'

'But what *are* these methods, Jethu?' There might have been a hint of impatience in my voice.

'Oh, there are several, and all roads lead to Rome,' Ghosh Jethu smiled as he settled back in the recliner. 'In fact, each of the spiritual traditions we know of, talks about some method or the other. There is, for instance, Tantra, which itself means "technique"; then there is Patanjali's Ashtanga Yog; there is Lahiri Mahasay's Kriya Yog; there is Tao, which means "path", "way" or "route"; there are the Sufi methods... You see Bhombol, it's actually a problem of plenty...'

'But if there be so many techniques to go beyond suffering, why should humanity still be in the state that it is in?' I was not convinced.

'See, you are already seeking the security of the intellect,' Ghosh Jethu laughed. 'You want an explanation. There could be many reasons, but why should you bother? As the great sage of Dakshineshwar, Ramakrishna Paramahansa, once said, you have come to the orchard to eat mangoes, why vex yourself with how many trees the orchard has, how many leaves, and so on? Eat your mangoes and be happy!'

The analogy appealed to me, and I said so.

'You see, the intellect can take you only thus far and no farther,' he continued. 'It cannot go beyond perception, beyond making inferences from what is already within one's range of experience. To take one beyond ordinary perception, the intellect is not the right vehicle. You need SPVs—special purpose vehicles, as an accountant would say—special techniques, to do that.'

'OK, so there are techniques. But how would one know if they actually work?'

'That should be simple Bhombol! Try a particular one sincerely for some time. If it yields the promised results, fine, continue with it. Otherwise, kick it out!'

'Well, Jethu, I can see I'm losing the argument, but I still can't quite buy your prescription. And as for Acharya Rajneesh, I've never had a fancy for him,' I said and both of us laughed.

'Assuming your assessment of Acharya Rajneesh is correct, which it is not,' Ghosh Jethu ran his fingers through his long grey hair as he resumed, 'remember one thing Bhombol: a broom, however dirty, never fails to clean. And talking of prescriptions, who am I to make out one for you? The hand that guides you in the dark is your own. You will come up with your own prescription once you've had some spiritual experience. You see, until one has tasted scotch, how should he be expected to give up country liquor?'

The comparison struck me like a bolt, reversing the course of time in a jagged flash, transporting me instantly to the moon-washed veranda of Shibuda's quarters in Jhargram, where a sparkling pair of neem-brushed canines beneath a bushy moustache welcomed my tiptoed steps even as two earthen tumblers brimming with fermented mahua promised a sojourn into the spirituous land of lofty delights.

I would perhaps have tarried a while longer in the land of my awakening, tottering amidst the profusion of sal, mahogany and mehul dazzling in the breezy full moon night, but for the tap on the back of my hand and Ghosh Jethu's gentle query if I was feeling all right.

'Oh yes,' I said, snapping out of the trance, 'I'm perfect.'

The conversation then turned to mundane things: whether I still disliked my lecturer's job, had someone to cook and wash for me, and if living alone was depressing. The last question would perhaps have led us to the subject of my separation with Sraboni, but an intruder had appeared on the scene.

The man who had opened the door for me was now standing at the door to the terrace, clearly waiting to say something. As Ghosh Jethu turned towards him enquiringly, the man mumbled something to the effect that dinner was ready to be served downstairs.

I looked at my ancient wristwatch and was startled to find the tiny radium-painted needles stationed at the advertiser-preferred 10.08—just a little over an hour before the last train back to Sealdah. Ghosh Jethu led me down to the ground floor where he showed me into a large room with peach walls, a white ceiling from which hung an ornate chandelier with complex arrays of crystal prisms, and a large round table with twelve gleaming tall-backs. At the far corner there stood an elegant white-ceramic wash basin, while a white hand towel dangled from a golden ring that the polished head of a ferocious brass tiger held between its locked jaws.

Ghosh Jethu made me sit first and took the chair at the other end of the diameter. His face, glowing in the refracted light of the chandelier, appeared to speak of some great satisfaction. The apologetic messenger now started bringing in the dishes one after the other until I voiced my alarm.

I had already counted fourteen when Ghosh Jethu smiled and said it was all right if I could not have all the dishes, but he would not let me off unless I had the prawns he had picked up especially for me, besides Barrackpore's famous sweet curd. I was touched. It must have been ages since anyone had lavished so much care on me.

The conversation at the dinner table was neither about my psychological status post-Sraboni, nor the parapsychological domains of Tantra or Tao. But the subject proved equally uneasy.

'Why don't you write to your parents more often? And what prevents you from visiting them at Ranchi once in a while?' Ghosh Jethu asked casually, even as I wrestled with the tiger prawn that refused to let go of its shell.

I could only mumble some excuse, which I knew was clearly unsatisfactory. But Ghosh Jethu did not persist with his query and kept quiet as I continued polishing off one dish after another. Finally, when I had excavated the last remnants of the sweet curd from the earthen pot, he looked straight into my eyes, declaring that there had been a purpose behind the summons to Barrackpore. I could still read nothing in his easy tone.

'Perhaps this is our last dinner together—the Last Supper, as it were,' his tone was matter-of-fact. 'But don't worry, I'm not going to get crucified after this,' he tried to joke seeing me sit up.

'But what? I mean, why?' My distress was evident.

'Well, first let us wash up and then I'll explain it all to you Bhombol. It will take some time, and I suggest you spend the night here with me.'

I was filled with foreboding.

'Tell me please,' I pleaded as soon as we had got into the drawing room.

'Don't be upset, Bhombol,' Ghosh Jethu tried reassuring me. 'It's just that I have found a Master.'

'What do you mean, found a master?'

'Well Bhombol, I have had my fill. A good job, money, social status, ancestral wealth, houses, servants... Besides, you see, I've merely gone through two of the four stages of the Vedic Ashram. Bramhacharya I have known and even Garhastya, with you as my son. Now it must be Vanaprastha, and may be Sanyas finally, provided I qualify for that and I live that long.'

'But where are you going?' I was frantic.

'I don't know Bhombol. I will go where my Master asks me to,' Ghosh Jethu's calm reply revealed nothing. Then, noticing my distress, he made an attempt at explaining:

'Are you familiar with Sri Sankaracharya's *Vivekachudamani*? I suppose you are not. In that, the founder of the Dasanami order of Hindu monks says there are three things that are indeed rare: a human birth, the desire for liberation, and the company of a perfected sage. And if you happen to have these three rare possessions, Sankara says, it is foolish for a man not to strive for self-liberation and kill himself by clinging to things that are unreal.'

I remained silent, making an effort to keep my emotions in check, then burst forth: 'I am ready to accept you still don't know where you will be going, but you can at least tell me who this person is—your master. And why is he taking you away?'

'Bhombol, I can see you are getting agitated,' Ghosh Jethu smiled. 'As a matter of fact, I don't know his name. The local people merely call him Baba. I met him at a short distance from Siliguri. During one of my long walks along the banks of Panchanoi. He has asked me to meet him again at that place on a certain date after I have settled all my affairs at home.'

I stood speechless, my eyes welling up and my right knee about to give away, even as a million angry questions and fuming protests threatened to explode in a deluge of livid outpourings. 'You have conned me!' I wanted to shout at the top of my voice.

I did nothing.

'There's one more thing, Bhombol,' Ghosh Jethu said, looking at me through his thick glasses in a strange way. He got up and went to the chest of drawers in one corner, and bringing out a leather folder, handed it over to me.

'I have distributed my property, in fact all my belongings, among various relatives. This house, I want to gift it to you. The relevant papers are all there in this folder.'

I threw the folder on the sofa and stormed out of Ghosh Bari.

The Garden of Eden

The last train from Barrackpore must have been held up somewhere midway, for it was past midnight by the time I emerged out of the sparsely occupied compartment to step onto the platform at Sealdah, still seething over Ghosh Jethu's heartless betrayal.

The only unrelated thought that had engaged me briefly during the depressing journey, like a comic recess in an otherwise unrelenting tragedy, was the recollection of my initial wonder at the name Sealdah when I had first transferred to Calcutta to get into Presidency College. A trickster of a senior at Hindu Hostel, a history buff, had informed the wide-eyed émigré from Ranchi that during British days, Sealdah was the place where foxes were routinely slaughtered and roasted before supply to Fort William, the army garrison on the eastern banks of the river. "Seyal" in Bangla means fox, and "dah" is to burn, which you perhaps know although you're a Bihari. And the stench was far too bad for even a Bihari to handle. Anyway, in documents of the Raj era, you'll find Sealdah mentioned as Foxburn, the name that New York City later plagiarised to name a street, just as they had earlier turned the name of the Vedic sage Angira into Niagra. You'll find all that in P.N. Oak's *World Vedic Heritage*,' he had informed me over tea and butter toast, sitting on a bare bench at the ward canteen. And I had fallen for the story hook, line and sinker. It was only when my acquired wisdom had been revealed to Ghosh Jethu with a flourish and he had burst out laughing that I realized the clueless 'Bihari' had been conned fair and square.

It could not have occurred to me then that one day he too would resort to a con job, leaving me broken and marooned.

Coming out of Sealdah station, I found the taxi stand completely deserted even as at the bus shelter a solitary vehicle revved, eager to depart. I got into it in a hurry, running the last few paces only to realize the revving was a trick to get dithering commuters to board quickly. I settled in a window seat to stare out at the rising flyover on the left, my mind raring to play back the events at Ghosh Bari just a little while ago. There were four or five persons other than me in the bus, all of them stone drunk and each a picture of staggering patience. The bus finally started off a good ten minutes later, unable to get in any more drunkards, and I sank back into the frayed rexine seat, my eyes burning even as a hammer pounded at my right temple.

The bus sped through the forsaken road, disregarding potholes, rumbling tramways, and irritable street dogs, braking heavily at stops to allow one spirituous master or the other to get off before resuming its rush through the eerie night. After some time, I realized there was no one else other than the conductor in the passenger cabin, and the thin rickety man with cropped hair and a deep scar on his cheek was leaning against a seat on the other side, jangling his bag of coins and asking me to get my ticket. I put my hand into my pocket and to my horror found the wallet missing. Frantically, I tried this pocket and that, but came up with only the key to my flat. Unnerved, I told the conductor I had either dropped my wallet somewhere or my pocket had been picked, and I would get off at my stop, rush to my flat and fetch him the fare. 'Which stop?' he asked me and when told it was Ballygunge Phari, he laughed on my face, saying the bus was headed in the opposite direction and that I should not have had that last swig. Left with no choice, I asked him to stop the bus, at which he lurched to the rear door, pulled the cord and as the bell in the driver's cabin clanked, the vehicle came to a screeching halt. I had to alight in the middle of nowhere.

Standing on the desolate stretch at that unearthly hour, I was at my wits' end. Looking around I realized I was on Harrison Road, and a brisk walk would take me to Bengal Renaissance College in about half an hour, where help could perhaps be found. Then it occurred to me that if I took a right immediately before the University of Calcutta I could well land up at my long-lost Garden of Eden—Eden Hindu Hostel—and perhaps spend the night there in the guest room if either Hoshiyarji or Thapada was still there. And if both had retired from service, or if they failed to recognise me, I would march up to Bengal Renaissance and wait there for some colleague or the other to arrive for the Sunday morning classes and bail me out.

A rapid walk soon brought me to the intersection of College Street and Peary Charan Sarkar Street, from where I turned right and within minutes stood before the massive century-old solid-wood gate of Government Eden Hindu Hostel. A dim naked bulb hung over it, serving to light up part of the approach and the white marble plaque on the red brick wall that proudly proclaimed in all caps: HERE LIVED DR RAJENDRA PRASAD/FIRST PRESIDENT OF INDIA/AS A STUDENT OF THE PRESIDENCY COLLEGE/BETWEEN JULY 1902 AND DECEMBER 1907. I had to bang on the gate for quite some time before a voice, the unmistakable voice, first cursed me in choice Bhojpuri and then asked me to hang on for a moment. Presently, the wicket was opened and as I cowered to squeeze in, there he was, Hoshiyarji, in his lungi and patched undershirt, eyes bloodshot, head almost bald, and his massive handlebar moustache the colour of snow. The ageing gatekeeper rubbed his eyes, blinked and let out a string of expletives blaming himself for having had a smoke too many—otherwise why the hell would the person before him look like Sudipto Babu! I told him I was Sudipto indeed, but he would not take my word for it. Getting into his tiny room adjacent to the gate, he brought out his brass pot, dabbed his face and eyes with water, and groaned that he was truly ruined—the goddamn apparition still looked like Sudipto Babu! But when I embraced him saying he was not mistaken, the old man could not hold back his tears.

'To be a man and yet to cry,' he mumbled, wiping his tears while ushering me into his little room. And as we sat on his charpoy after Hoshiyarji had yanked off the mosquito net, he asked me how was it that I had chosen to visit him after so many years and at such an hour. I had to say it was my lost wallet that had brought me to his doorstep, and he laughed, saying wallets were meant to be lost and he did not care for it, but was really and truly sorry for what had been a rather crude welcome address. I did not care for his address too, I said; his tears had whispered to me all I needed to know. Hoshiyarji blushed at the mention of tears but was quick to parry, reminding me how I too had cried copiously on the day of Saraswati puja—so what if that was some twenty years back?—and what a scene I had created at the hostel gate!

Hoshiyarji was indeed right. It was actually the day after Saraswati puja, and a group of us hostelites along with Hoshiyarji had hired a lorry and gone over to Babughat to immerse the idol of the Goddess who had been, just the previous day, fervently petitioned by many a shirking student to save him from flunking some impending examination or another. There was a long queue of 'immersionists' ahead of us and as we awaited our turn at the riverbank, Hoshiyarji spotted a man selling kulfi at a distance. The two of us had gone up to him and asked him what flavours he had, at which the kulfi seller had first peered at us and then, after the other customers had left, told us in a low voice that he did have green cannabis balls to serve with the kulfi.

I was a bit hesitant initially, but at Hoshiyarji's reassurance decided to try out the green balls along with the kulfi. When I'd had at least four, Hoshiyarji asked me to stop, but I would not listen and casually remarked that the stuff had either nothing in it or too little. At that, the kulfi seller, who had overheard me, got quite agitated and offered me a fistful free, saying if that did not knock me off I was free to name a mongrel after him. Hoshiyarji tried to draw me away, but I had already had quite a few by then. The mischief over, we trudged back to join our group, which had meanwhile moved ahead in the queue.

It was only about half an hour or so later, while we were still awaiting our turn for the immersion, that the cannabis hit me. Suddenly, I had the chilling idea that the river was creeping towards us and would soon wash me away. Panic-stricken, I caught hold of Hoshiyarji's arm and begged him to save me, declaring pitifully that I was the only child of my parents and could not swim. Realizing I was beginning to attract attention, Hoshiyarji pulled me aside and dragged me away from the queue, telling the others that we needed to find a loo in a hurry. I was hauled to the bus stop nearby, forced into a moseying vehicle into which Hoshiyarji hopped in too, but by the time we were dropped off at College Street, I was on the verge of a breakdown. Now it was not the river chasing me, but the fear I would turn mad, most certainly and irretrievably, very soon. It was with great difficulty that Hoshiyarji got me to the hostel gate, I later heard, but the farce had yet to climax.

The moment we got into the hostel I spotted Mrinalini standing near the steps, clad in a dazzling white sari, flowers in her hair, smiling at me, and holding a packet of oranges and chocolate. She had come to visit me in all goodness, the day being a Sunday. But I was in no shape to appreciate that. I stared at her for some time, marvelling at her resemblance to the Goddess I had just abandoned by the river, and broke into inconsolable sobs, blubbering wretchedly that I was turning mad and seeing Mrinalini everywhere. For some time Hoshiyarji consoled me saying everything would be all right soon, but was eventually overwhelmed by my misery and the cannabis that he too had swallowed in generous doses. That rogue of a kulfi seller had poisoned us both, he declared, and we were now destined forever to see Mrinalini Madam everywhere, in land, sea and air, he bawled, as we stood at the hostel entrance locked in an embrace like long-lost brothers just united. We would have gone on with our shrill lament, but it suddenly dawned on me that Hoshiyarji had no bloody right to see Mrinalini anywhere since she was my sweetheart. The thought first sent me into a stupor, but I was out of it in no time, breathing fire and threatening to kill the poor man if he did not forthwith stop seeing Mrinalini Madam—here, there or wherever.

That day some otherwise indifferent souls in the hostel had been kind enough to intervene, get us into our respective rooms and see off a stunned Mrinalini at the university bus stop with the reassurance that we would be ourselves when the cannabis wore off.

'Babu, did you marry Mrinalini Madam after all?' Hoshiyarji broke into my reverie.

'I had intended to, but Mrinalini found someone else and married him,' I kept my reply brief. The old man's face fell and he remained silent, staring at the floor.

'Then like me you haven't married at all?' he asked after a while, his handlebar drooping and his face a portrait of misery.

'I did marry eventually,' I said, 'although maybe I should not have. But in any case, my wife also left me sometime back, taking with her our daughter, and here I am a bumbling bachelor once again, after a long time.'

Hoshiyarji grew thoughtful, gazing out of the window and running his hand over his tattered pillow. Coming around, he turned his bloodshot eyes at me and said that my ability to accept adversity in life was God's gift, a rare gift indeed. And then, looking away, he added, 'But Babu, you should take care never to defile the gift with anger, no matter what the provocation.'

The comment struck me as odd and I would have quizzed him on it, but we were interrupted by loud banging on the hostel gate and several voices calling out for Hoshiyarji in turns.

Both of us hurried out and as Hoshiyarji opened the wicket, three young men trooped in, smelling of liquor and spices, full of good-natured laughter and somewhat unsteady on their legs.

'Which hell are you returning from?' Hoshiyarji demanded in Bhojpuri, but in reply one of the young men bowed low before him saying sorry over and over again, straightened up and pinched the old man's cheek telling him he was a darling and looked very sweet when upset. Another said they had been partying at a friend's place at Shyambazar and by the time the merrymaking was over there was no bus or taxi available; so they had to walk all the way back. Then, noticing me, the third chap, who had been standing at a distance smiling all the while, asked Hoshiyarji in a clearly audible whisper if I was from the police and whether the hostel superintendent had hatched some plot to fix boarders returning late at night.

Hoshiyarji laughed out loud and said I was Sudipto Babu, the same that they had heard so much about, the college and university rank holder, and the college badminton champion for three years in a row. Yes, I was the one who hailed from Bihar, Hoshiyarji's native place, and was the best friend he had ever had in his long and worthless career opening and closing the goddamn gate to admit or eject drunkards at Government Eden Hindu Hostel.

'Oh, Detective Sudipto!' the three musketeers exclaimed almost in unison and promptly thrust their hands at me. I had to shake them one after the other, wondering if it was actually so very long ago that I too had been like these blissful young men, with nary a care in the world.

'But why detective?' I asked the tipsy trio and Hoshiyarji bit his tongue. Hanging his head and staring at his own feet he kept muttering to himself, finally looking up at me to say it was simply beyond him how I could ever forget the ghost who used to trouble Pushpita Babu of Ward 1. He had told the boys the story, he confessed.

I could immediately recall the incident, but kept my mouth shut. At that Hoshiyarji grew frantic, and in all innocence began to offer cues: Did I not remember, I was the prefect of Ward 1 then? I had not yet shifted to the single seater in Ward 5. Did that ring a bell?

It was impossible not to smile. And with that there was no escape. The three young men, all on a high, began pleading with me, saying providence had arranged my visit to the hostel and they would not let the opportunity of hearing the story from the detective himself slip by at any cost.

I had to give in. We moved to the ward canteen where the three men and Hoshiyarji promptly planted themselves on the floor while I was made to sit on the bench—the same that had been forced to mutely suffer, over the course of perhaps a century, many a rambling story at the most absurd of hours.

Room 6 in Ward 1 at Hindu Hostel in our times had a reputation for oddity, I began. It was a four-seater, untidy even by our hostel standards, and was at that time occupied by three philosophy undergraduates, each a scaled up or downsized version of the other, and all of them self-certified soul mates. Trouble began when as the ward prefect I got a fourth person, a diminutive first-year botany student, Pushpita Ranjan Ghoroi, into the vacant fourth seat. Pushpita, who came from Bengal's scholarly district Midnapore, carried with him his remote village in his dress, speech and demeanour. He also suffered from some form of night-blindness and was mortally scared of ghosts. The trouble was, his roommates, town cats all, were not too keen to have amongst them a 'half-blind villager' who moreover had a girlish first name. The hapless boy's plea that he be called by his masculine middle name, Ranjan, cut no ice with them.

Now, these roommates, eager to have Pushpita shifted out of their bastion, had cooked up the story that a few years back a love-smitten botany student had hanged himself from the ceiling fan of that very room and since then whenever anyone who had anything to do with botany tried staying in Room 6, he was destined to die before long in the most mysterious of circumstances. Even talking about the incident could invoke the malevolent force, Pushpita was warned.

Initially, Pushpita, gullible though he was, had taken the story with a pinch of salt. But when his roommates went home during the Durga Puja holidays leaving him alone in the four-seater, the poor boy began to grow apprehensive. At the ward canteen, he would talk of hearing strange noises at night, as if someone was whistling, but I had paid no heed. However, things came to a head one day when he woke me up well past midnight, banging on my door and howling, 'Prefect dada, please save my life. Oh, please save my life, I beg you… Someone is killing me.' I jumped out of bed and was quite unnerved to find him trembling at my door, his vest drenched in tears and sweat, and his lungi about to slip down. I pulled him in, latched the door and switched on the lights. It took Pushpita quite some time to calm down, but when he did, the terrified boy told me something so preposterous that I've still not got over it even after all these years. 'Prefect dada,' he stammered between gasps, his hands still shaking, 'someone without a body sneaks into my room every night and blows on my anus. He wants to kill me.'

The three young men were rolling on the floor clutching their stomach even as Hoshiyarji sat silent, his hands raised and his mouth open, but his large tummy in frenzied vibration, threatening to shake down his patched undershirt. I had held back for long the gale of laughter rising within, but Hoshiyarji's strange pose was simply too much to handle.

'Then?' one of the students panted, although I was certain he knew the story by heart.

Well, I had to turn Sherlock Holmes, I said, so pitiable was Pushpita's condition. The problem was I could not consult anyone, for if I did, the story would be out and poor Pushpita would be ragged to death. I could clearly see the next issue of our wall magazine featuring a box item with the caption 'Anus Horribilis' if the word got around. Fortunately, even I was alone in my room that day, my roommates having gone home for Durga

Puja, and no one got to know. That is, except Hoshiyarji, who was sworn to secrecy.

I began sleeping in Pushpita's room that night on, hoping to catch the bizarre blower in the act, but the prankster seemed to have simply vanished. Soon, it so turned out that Pushpita, reassured by my presence, would be snoring away to glory all night, while I would be lying awake with a torch beside my pillow and Hoshiyarji's stout stick next to the bed, although perfectly aware that a full grown man could never be killed by blowing on his rump.

The mystery was finally solved on the seventh day. I discovered that the door to Room 6 had a large keyhole, and on windy nights, gusts of air would blow straight into Pushpita's bed, often making a faint whistling sound. And invariably, the hapless fellow would have his lungi rolled up to the waist while asleep, his rear directly exposed to the gusty assault. Nothing would happen during the day since the door would remain open then.

The three young men laughed for a long time and soon began asking for more anecdotes, at least 'one for the road'. 'Which road?' I asked, and they were quick to admit there was none, but still wanted another story. Thankfully, Hoshiyarji intervened, saying I was tired, having walked all the way from Harrison Road, and after some cajoling managed to pack off the trio. Turning to me, he said not much was left of the night and offered to show me into the first-floor guest room after fetching the keys.

Trudging up the century-old wooden stairs I followed Hoshiyarji to Ward 2, dimly lit by a row of unwilling yellow bulbs and walked the long familiar corridor to get to the corner that was fenced off by chicken wire and a gate. Hoshiyarji opened the gate, and unlocking the large green door of the guest room, switched on the lights. Stepping out, he stood at the threshold and bowed in a gesture of welcome, a smile curving up from beneath his snow white handlebar.

It was as if the old custodian, the lone survivor of the ages, had so long held in his loving arms what had once been my home for five eventful years, consoling it every now and then, whispering in its ears the reassurance that I would turn up some day, unannounced, at the dead of night, to fill it with my being and convey to it in unspoken words what profits I had made and what losses, what new lands I had seen and what people, over the years and decades—before heaving a sigh and rising once again, at the hint of the morning twilight, to tie my shoelaces and trudge off into the misty future, leaving behind just the faint half-promise that maybe, if the stars acquiesced, I would perhaps return, briefly, in an encore of the moment at hand.

Would I not enter? Hoshiyarji had been asking, but I had not heard him. And when I did, it occurred to me I should share with the old man the relative comforts of the guest room for the few hours that were left of the night. Why couldn't he stay with me when there were two large beds? He said that was out of the question, and moreover, there would have to be someone at the main gate. Couldn't he ask one of the ward boys to sleep in his room? I would not give up, and neither would he relent. Finally, it is when I made a long face and said I was looking forward to a smoke with him after so many years that he began to waver.

Eventually, Hoshiyarji decided he would wake up Thapada's nephew—who was filling in for his vacationing uncle—and ask the young man to spend the rest of the night at the gate. The solution found, he made to hurry, promising to return in a moment with the essentials—joints of grass, his brass pot, and his own pillow, without which he could not sleep. And as for the impropriety of smoking pot in the guest room, there had been many a precedence, he added on his way out although I had not raised the issue.

The guest room, I noticed, had remained the same: two large beds, a wooden almirah in a corner, a secretariat table with a thick glass top and a chair, an ancient DC fan with four blades, and a large easy chair by the curtain-less window. The additions since my time were an ashtray and a reading lamp on the secretariat table, and on the wall facing the table, a large notice board, which displayed a typed sheet listing out the rules of occupation along with a wall magazine, more than a year old.

It was the calligraphy on the magazine that caught my eye. And as I went over to take a closer look, the name Sudipto leapt out of it. The magazine had, besides a few empty poems in blank verse, an article by one Sudipto Das, in which he argued passionately why the leitmotif 'Lara's Theme' in the Omar Sharif-starrer *Doctor Zhivago*, would have been better served by Al Martino's 'Somewhere My Love'. The lyrics of the song, which to his regret had been composed much after the release of the film, had been reproduced:

Somewhere my love, there will be songs to sing
Although the snow covers the hope of spring.
Somewhere a hill, blossoms in green and gold,
And there are dreams, all that your heart can hold.
Someday, we'll meet again my love,
Someday, whenever the Spring breaks through...
You'll come to me out of the long ago,
Warm as the wind, soft as the kiss of snow.
Till then my sweet, think of me now and then,
God speed our love, till you are mine again...

'Who did you marry that she left you?' It was Hoshiyarji, standing at the green door, packing grass in a clay pipe with his thumb and staring at me with strange kindly eyes.

'Sraboni,' I replied, wondering if he would remember her from our MA days when she would visit me sometimes at the hostel. To my surprise he did. Hoshiyarji could clearly recall the tall and fair madam with long hair who would drop in now and then asking for me, and in fact remembered her distress when told that my parents had taken me away from the hostel after I had been laid ill by some wrong medicine.

Hoshiyarji lit his clay pipe and passed it on to me. I took a drag as I joined him on the floor, locked in the smoke for a while and exhaled. Memories came tumbling in: those long sessions at the hostel grounds sitting on Hoshiyarji's sagging charpoy; the adventures of Raja Begum; the vivid descriptions of the forests of Hazaribagh, and of Ranchi, the land of lakes and waterfalls; the first invitation to Jhargram via a telephone call... A couple of drags more and it was now Hoshiyarji's turn at the pipe. The veteran pulled long and hard, held for an eternity, and finally breathed out. Gradually a mist came over his large red eyes, and he could not hold back what must have been troubling him for some time.

It had never occurred to him I was in love with Sraboni, he remarked, and after a pause let loose a volley of questions: Why should a miserable fate have to be mine all the time? First a dislocating knee and now a wife who runs away with the kid! Why was it that whoever Hoshiyarji cared for ended up in misery? Why was it that I had not come to him earlier and told him of my problems? Why had I not asked him to offer sugar and green coconut at the Thanthania Kalibari down Bidhan Sarani? Did I not know of his special relationship with the Goddess? Had he not told me how Maa Kali would watch over him every time he went into the tiger-infested Hazaribagh forest with Raja Begum?

I could not help feeling sorry for Hoshiyarji. Here indeed was the person Dadu should have written about—a simple, artless soul, an ordinary gatekeeper, who possessed nothing in the world except the rarest of qualities: goodness, plain goodness. It was evident he was crying, and I looked away so as not to embarrass him. But as I turned towards the wall, my eyes fell upon a fragment of the verse on the notice board.

You'll come to me out of the long ago,
Warm as the wind, soft as the kiss of snow.
Till then my sweet, think of me now and then...

Somewhere deep within, a river in sudden spate washed an embankment away, but not a word was uttered, not a sigh heaved. I kept staring at the notice board, watching the green velvet gradually turn into an illumined screen, and present in trembling detail the play of light and shade beneath the swaying foliage of the sal, mahogany and neem, the flickering shapes on the lime-washed walls of a forest bungalow lit up by a fitful lantern on a long winter night, and the bewitching contours of a chiselled face, inviting, mysterious, staring through the pattern of obovate moon-dusted cashew leaves...

'Did Sraboni Madam know about Mrinalini Madam? Before the wedding? Did you tell her yourself, Babu?' Hoshiyarji's voice almost broke. He was too far gone into my predicament to remember propriety. His gnarled hand touched mine as I struggled with the tide within.

The old man's overflowing concern washed away whatever inhibition I had about talking of Sraboni's entry into my life. I let down my guard and opened up as never before, recounting everything as I relived it.

She knew everything about Mrinalini, I said. In fact, I had even told Sraboni I should not be marrying her, but things had spun out of hand once I was away in Delhi, having found employment there. Left to myself and into my first job, I would write frequently to my mentor, Ghosh Jethu, at Ranchi, complaining of hostility and humiliation in office and seeking his advice in every little thing. My parents, especially my mother, having come to know of my torments and fearing that I would lapse into depression, had in secret sought out Sraboni in Calcutta and finding her still unmarried pleaded with her to save me from wasting away. My mother had insisted that she, being a woman, knew beyond doubt my affection for Sraboni was deep, and that even my doctor had said so on many occasions. In fact, according to my mother, the psychiatrist had even remarked that Sraboni was perhaps the only person who could get me back to my old happy ways since she had my trust—provided she came into my life once again.

Initially, Sraboni had fought the idea off, but my mother's repeated assurance that my affection for Sraboni was abiding, persuaded her to consider the proposition. But she said she would decide only after having had a word with me in person and in private, in Calcutta.

I had been unaware of all this, being in Delhi, and had come down to Calcutta unsuspectingly at my parents' behest. It was only when I was told Sraboni would be visiting me the following day at the very place we had put up, the AG Bengal guesthouse at Kidderpore, that I smelt a rat. But it was too late to do anything.

The interview proved fateful. Sraboni turned up the next morning somewhat pale and unsure, her long dark hair gathered in a bun and her eyes downcast. Spotting her from my first-floor window, I rushed down and saw her follow the peon into the visitor's room. I hesitated for a moment before entering it, watching her as she seated herself in the corner double-seater and wiped her forehead with a crushed handkerchief. She was wearing a white and pink salwar-kameez, but it seemed a size too large for her.

Sraboni looked up the moment I walked in, made to get up but decided against it, and offered a weak smile instead. I too faced a moment of awkwardness, not knowing how to begin. Marching up to the air conditioner that was already spouting chilled air in clouds of mist, I fiddled with the temperature knob for a while before I turned towards Sraboni.

'How are you doing?' I asked, unable to find a better opening.

'I'm fine,' she replied somewhat defensively and remained silent, looking away from me. Knowing a dead end loomed ahead, I took the initiative once again.

'You look unwell, and a great deal thinner. Is everything all right with you Sraboni?'

Perhaps it was the wrong question to ask. Sraboni wound and unwound her handkerchief around her fingers for some time and then shot back, 'What is it that you want to know?'

I tried to change tack, 'I'm so happy you came. Thought I would never see you again.'

She kept fidgeting with her handkerchief and after a long pause asked, 'And how are you doing?'

I told her I had made great progress since my failed suicide bid just before the MA finals—yes, it was a suicide bid, I repeated on hearing her gasp, not a wrong medicine taken by mistake as Hoshiyarji had broadcast. Then I told her of my job in Delhi, how I was making money out of dotting the i's and crossing the t's.

Sraboni lapsed into silence once again, seemingly weighing various options. Then collecting herself, she asked, 'Have you been able to get over Mrinalini?'

I had not anticipated this, but there was no hesitation when I said, 'No. Not fully yet. But I have made good progress.'

She was taken aback. After staring at my face for some time, she turned away and fixed her sights on the potted areca palm in the corner. It was after ages she emerged out of her thoughts: 'You remain honest as ever, no matter what your other failings.'

The peon brought in two tall glasses of soft drinks and a plate of cashew nuts, probably at the instructions of my mother. 'Have some,' I offered and Sraboni picked up a glass.

I waited till she had taken a sip of the chilled orange drink and then came out with the question I knew I had to ask her.

'Tell me, Sraboni, is it you who wanted to see me or was it my mother who made you come here?'

'Both,' she said after some thought.

'You remain honest too, no matter what your other strengths,' I quipped.

For the first time since her visit, Sraboni smiled. And then, as if realizing she had made an error, grew serious instantly. Putting her glass down on the centre table and looking me in the eye she fired point blank: 'Do you think I should marry you as your mother wants?'

It was again my turn to be startled. But it did not take me time to bring myself to say no.

'No,' I repeated emphatically, adding, 'because there is a grave mismatch between what I perhaps need and what you deserve: I need a crutch, you deserve a husband—a real husband. Sraboni, I love you too much to be able to use you as a crutch.'

She turned her face away with a jerk and I could well make out a battle had broken out within. A minute into the struggle and she bit her lip, covered her face with her dupatta and broke into muffled sobs.

Not knowing what to do I went over and sat beside her on the sofa, running my hand on her head, asking her not to be upset and apologising for having brought all this upon her.

'Then?' Hoshiyarji grew impatient, as I paused to take a swig from his brass pot. His clay pipe had long gone out, but he did not care to light it.

Sraboni sobbed for a while, I resumed, before calming down and confessed that she had been unable to get over our brief romance. She had turned down several marriage proposals and did not know how to live the rest of her life. She said the breakdown of our relationship had left her crippled and she would never be able to live with anyone else. Besides, even if she did tie the knot with some stranger, would it not be unfair to him!

'Can you not give me just a single chance, Sudipto? Mrinalini is married and gone, isn't it?' Sraboni looked up at me, her tear-smeared face pitching me headlong into another fateful day, several years back, into another room of the same guest house. I was a branded psycho case then, staring into the abyss, begging the unyielding beloved not to let go of me, not to let the mistaken supposition that I would hold the past against her loosen her grip, not to let me topple over and hurtle down into the dark depths never to rise again. Let us give it a try, I had pleaded with Mrinalini repeatedly, in a vain attempt to have her hand in marriage, assuring her over and over again that even if it did not work—an impossibility—the rear exit was always there. But by then she had found another hand to hold.

I turned my gaze at Sraboni, realizing my life had come full circle. I was on the stage again, the same stage, in the same house of horrors, participating in the same play; only my role had changed from that of the petitioner to the petitioned. But this time the outcome was in my hands. True, I could not avert the tragedy, or the fate of the chief tragedian, but I could nevertheless alter the script. And cut down the toll by half: from two to one.

Taking in a deep breath, I said yes. Yes, I would marry her and forget Mrinalini.

Hoshiyarji wiped a tear and let out a sigh as I took another swig from his brass pot. For a few minutes the old man kept silent, but he had not yet asked the last of his questions.

'Why did Sraboni Madam leave you then, Sudipto Babu?'

'Because in life we think something and something else happens,' I answered. 'I had been unable to keep my resolve, and had failed to stop myself from dwelling on Mrinalini now and then.'

The hint of dawn was stealing in through the wooden slats of the two windows in the guest room at the Garden of Eden: time to tie the shoelaces and trudge off into the misty road ahead.

The Retreat

It was pouring on the plains. And on the hills. But it had stopped raining within. Long back. Ever since the forced parting with Ghosh Jethu—an event that had inured the Sisyphus in me to the curse of recurrent failure in matters of the heart, both romantic and otherwise. Or so had been my conjecture then.

The drive from Delhi to Pangot via Gajraula and then Nainital, in a borrowed car, was like a journey through endless panes of water. But I persisted like a rally driver, indifferent to the thud of potholes and the swish of the wipers, determined to cover the vain expanse of some three hundred kilometres without a breakdown.

My visit to Delhi had been on the invitation of Sunil Jain, my erstwhile colleague at Indus Software & Advisory Services. Sunil, who was still with the company recruiting 'original thinkers', had been suffering from bipolar disorder since his wife Maya's accidental death and wanted my company for a few days if that did not greatly inconvenience me—a request I did not have the heart to turn down. It was at Sunil's trans-Yamuna house while we were reliving those good old days at Indus before it went public that Mrinalini tracked me down, on Facebook, which I had joined recently out of sheer desperation. My elderly online bridge partner had just thrown in the cards, and after mourning the loss for months I had signed up with the social networking site hoping to fish out some old Contract hand from the virtual world presumably teeming with former boarders of Eden Hindu Hostel. But the net delivered a catch of Mrinalini instead.

'Hands up! You're under arrest. Turn over your numbers now,' she had posted on my wall. Initially I was taken aback, but then drew some relief from the fact that I kept no cell phones and had even surrendered my landline connection years back (opting for a no-frills broadband link instead). I had nothing to turn over, I wrote back, adding, with some satisfaction, that I was not to be found in Calcutta but in Delhi, at a friend's place on a holiday.

It was the needless addendum that did me in. Mrinalini got back instantly, saying she and her daughter would be passing through the city in the next two days on their way to Pangot for a brief vacation. And they would be greatly pleased and immensely grateful if I could meet them at Pangot the following long weekend. It had been her daughter's wish for long that she get to meet me at least once, having heard so much about my antics in college.

I was quite hesitant and sought Sunil's counsel, but he said the lady's request was not too difficult to keep. In fact, he went a step further lending me his car for the drive to Pangot, along with directions, a detailed road map, and good wishes. 'Pangot is a beautiful place, just a couple of cliffs away from Nainital, at the Kumaon foothills of the outer Himalayas. It's a bird watcher's paradise. You'll love it. I too would have gone with you, but it was Maya's favourite,' he said.

Before leaving Delhi, I had been informed that a cottage had been 'booked' and all arrangements made for the meeting at Pangot. The date, a national holiday—the fifteenth of August. It was a Friday. I would spend the next day at Pangot and drive back to Delhi on Sunday. The following Monday I would be home again—back in Calcutta to carry on with the pointless job of fitting square pegs into round holes.

I had tried to resist the idea of revisiting the past amidst the hills, suggesting we visit Jhargram instead sometime in the (uncommitted) future, but Mrinalini had shot down the proposal, writing: 'Jhargram, never! Will talk about it when we meet.'

It would be eighteen years to the day I would be meeting Mrinalini again. Eighteen years since her hasty marriage to a charming hotel colleague. But the charm had not lasted very long. An employee verification drive by the luxury hotel in the wake of a terrorist threat had led to investigations and the otherwise frank gentleman was found to have faked his basic qualifications. Prompt eviction followed, both from the workplace and from the Shyambazar home, which had come into Mrinalini's joint possession after her father passed away, leaving a regretful wife who sought distraction in her growing granddaughter. For Mrinalini, the rift this breach of trust had created proved too wide even for the sacred contract of marriage to bridge.

I had known of the incident for long, one of my schoolmates from Ranchi being in the hospitality industry and a supplier of upholstery to the Wanderlust Luxury Hotel in Calcutta. The story had not been published anywhere; apparently, it was not newsworthy enough.

The stretch from Nainital to Pangot, a distance of some fifteen kilometres, proved arduous. The thin winding road with several hairpins was full of pebbles and craters, and the incline quite steep. I went up at a crawling pace, all the time fearing that the next turn would pitch me headlong against some manic vehicle hurtling down. That would be the end of a chequered albeit news-unworthy life, which my obituary in the *Bengal Renaissance* would perhaps ruefully describe as one that had been full of ups and downs, the final down, of several hundred feet, proving fatal. But I had waded so far through water that were I to wade no more, returning would be more tedious than crawling up—to a solitary cottage perched on top of a lonesome rock.

A wooden board nailed to an unusually large rhododendron declared in bold italics, **The Retreat, Pangot**; a sickly hand-drawn arrow resembling a fish skeleton underscored the name, providing direction. I had to go ahead some 20 metres up to the next curve to find a grass verge where I parked the car, the wheels on the driver's side resting on the very edge. Getting off from the other side I found myself completely drenched in no time. I picked up my ancient haversack from the boot and trudged along the track that the signboard pointed at and soon faced the large wooden door of The Retreat.

A manservant ushered me in, expressing sympathy at my dripping frame, and showed me to my room on the first floor, saying 'madam' would meet me over lunch in another fifteen minutes. 'Which madam?' I let off one of my brainless ones and was promptly informed in a somewhat hushed tone it was Madam Mrinalini from Calcutta, the owner. The tiny radium-painted hands of my old wristwatch peering through a misty glass lid said it was 2.30 p.m. already. Mrinalini and her daughter would have been starving.

I quickly changed into dry clothes, patted down my wet hair, and was about to rush downstairs when I caught a fleeting glimpse of myself on the dressing table mirror. My heart sank. The man on the other side, though somewhat familiar, could have featured in any of Bollywood's ketchup-splashed horror movies without makeup. But what was the remedy? I darted into the wash room, shaved, combed my hair carefully and rubbed some cream all over my face, prompting the large oval basin mirror to throw back an oily fluorescent countenance, glowing in the soft bluish-white light of the small coiled CFL.

I descended the flight of wooden stairs slowly, placing the dignity of full eighty kilos on every step, but having reached the ground floor did not know which way to turn. Summoning my olfactory faculties to guide me to the table, I followed the trail of an appetising whiff, pushed open a door and made a grand entry into a fairly large room that turned out to be the kitchen. Two liveried men jumped up, one holding a wooden spatula and the other a kitchen knife, and hitting their foreheads with their implements cried out 'Namashkar sir' in unison. I was then conducted into the dining room where I found Mrinalini seated in a large wooden chair, her elbows on the table and her chin resting on her palms.

Eighteen years had slipped away irretrievably since I had last stepped uneasily into unfamiliar surroundings to stand before a seated Mrinalini, my eyes, of dry rubies, unable to acknowledge the person fidgeting on her right. It had been an August 15 rain-drenched evening at Parish Hall in the throbbing heart of Calcutta. The occasion, her wedding reception. I had been transported there along with several friends from college, clasping with both my sweating hands a cellophane-wrapped *Banalata Sen*. Initially I had thought I would give away my copy to Mrinalini, considering she would borrow it every time she went holidaying to her grandpa's at Jhargram during that age of innocence, brief and long mislaid. But then had eventually picked up a later reprint from a College Street bookstore, counselling myself that a new beginning warranted a new book, not one steeped in associations.

'There you are!' Mrinalini exclaimed as she looked up startled, while the girl sitting on her right chirped 'Hello', getting up from her chair.

'Hi! You look good... both of you,' I said, determined not to be caught dumb, pulling up a heavy chair somewhat clumsily opposite Mrinalini's.

'Keep standing! Let me take a look,' Mrinalini commanded. I had to agree, much to the amusement of the teenaged onlooker.

'You have put on weight! My God, you've started greying too! Oh I'm so glad you came! Gunjan, here's our famous Sudipto you've been dying to meet. A college and university rank holder, and a former badminton champion, but with a rattling knee...'

'Oh no Mom, that was unkind! You too have creaking knees,' Gunjan protested.

Planting myself firmly in the chair and in the present I turned my gaze towards Mrinalini. I noted that she was waging a losing battle against time, notwithstanding the generous help from the cosmetics industry that was now reporting annual growth rates in excess of 20 per cent in India, according to a recent PTI take. Mrinalini had added greatly to her circumference and now bore a striking resemblance to her mother, sporting almost the same pair of kohl-lined watery eyes, the same curved nose and the same thin mouth that appeared to hint at a streak of cold unconcern. And she too appeared to be some kind of a former empress—one who could switch between charming politeness and assertiveness with effortless ease. Mrinalini's daughter, on her part, carried no similarities with the mother, although the original eyes had been reprinted in the newer edition.

The lunch was an elaborate affair. But the dishes were unusual. There was a mishmash of assorted vegetables, brinjal fritters, lentil soup, chicken curry, egg curry and thick brown rice. It was only when I came to the double-yolk eggs that I realized Jhargram was being relived.

'Shibuda's menu!' I exclaimed, as two yolks rolled out, whisking me into in a world of scarlet, blue and emerald green. Lofty trees stood all around—sal, neem, mahogany, mehul—and as I dream-walked barefoot on the red earth, a figure seemed to emerge in the distance where an azure sky merged with the vaporous green of treetops. Gradually, as the figure drew closer, I could clearly see an old gentleman with a shock of silky white hair, round glasses and a benign smile—a smile that was still an anodyne, soothing the bruises of inexorable circumstance with the caress of memory. 'Dadu!' I would perhaps have called out, but for Mrinalini.

'Oh we are relieved!' she said, breaking the spell. 'Gunjan had no doubt you would be able to connect to Jhargram, but I was not so sure. In fact, she is the one who had the raw materials brought all the way post-haste from the Garh Salboni market.'

I gathered myself, smiled gratefully at Gunjan and asked Mrinalini why she wasn't sure of my reaction.

'Because you always get caught up in unnecessary details,' she said simply.

I did not understand what she meant, but sought no clarification.

Lunch over, we moved into the large living room. The lights had not been switched on and it was somewhat dark. Outside, the rain had stopped but the bay windows still showed an overcast sky. I was about to settle down in a single sofa opposite Mrinalini's, a dead wood centre table between us, when Gunjan sprang on her toes. 'Come Uncle, let me show you around,' she gushed, 'this is a lovely place too, although quite different from Jhargram.'

A hint of disappointment stole into some corner within, but I would not put a damper on the young girl's enthusiasm and followed her, as I would perhaps have Titir, as she darted about from one place to another.

'Isn't this a lovely place?' Gunjan asked, after she had taken me in and out of three spacious bedrooms on the ground floor, each with a double bed, a large wooden wardrobe, an ornate dressing table, a writing desk, and a wall-mounted LCD television set. 'The kitchen's in the other flank, and behind that are the staff quarters,' she said, adding, 'Your bedroom on the first floor is my favourite!'

'I see,' I nodded, but she pursed her lips and complained, 'But there's no terrace.' And then, lugging me by the hand ventured outdoors. 'Look at that,' she said excitedly, pointing to a lawn about the size of a tennis court with trees and flowering plants all around. 'It's Kikuyu grass; you find that in the heights,' she smiled, and in the next instant, embarked on a rapid-fire commentary, telling me of the names of the various trees and flowers, calling my attention to this one's colour and that one's shape even as the rumblings of distant waves of a different era, different shore, threatened to upset the delicate tranquillity of the moment.

'Where did you pick up so much from?' I asked Gunjan, collecting myself.

She beamed, triumphant. Then pointing into the distance said, 'Look at those dark hills through the pattern of leaves. Imagine the sight when the skies are blue.'

'With tufts of white wind-rushed clouds floating by,' I smiled.

'Yes!' she was now ecstatic. 'Mom says you're a poet wasted on a prosaic job. And she says of you, "Give him a tree or a creeper and a piece of sky and he will forget everything else. 'Madhabilata' (Rangoon creeper) is more precious to him than Madhabi,"' she giggled.

'Really?' was all I could say, wondering what else Mrinalini might have told her daughter about me.

'Have you been to Jhargram?' I asked Gunjan at length, 'I mean recently?'

'Recently? No. But I visited the place with Mom a number of times. Before the property was sold off.'

'Sold off? Why?' I was shocked.

'After great grandpa passed away, a forest fire reduced his bungalow to ashes... You didn't know? Shibukaka also left to return to his village. Eventually, Mom did build a small cottage there and had the whole estate fenced at considerable cost, but there was no one to look after the property and it was wasting away. With no one living there, the whole place was taken over by criminals. Mom had even gone to the police, but they said their hands were tied. It's a long story. Mom will give you the details. In fact, we were quite lucky to have found a buyer, although the price we got was shameful—that's what Mom says. And she says, "Pangot is my new Jhargram; it's been worth the price."'

Jhargram sold off? I could not hold back my disappointment and suggested that we save the rest of the conducted tour for some later time and return to the living room.

'Conducted tour!' Gunjan laughed as she led me back into the living room where a thoughtful Mrinalini reclining against a bolster with a volume of Neruda next to her awaited our return. I plumped into a sofa and was about to enquire about the sale of Dadu's bungalow when Mrinalini asked, 'You remember Dadu's big fat diary, don't you?'

'Of course!' I replied, and after some thought added, 'But I had sent it back to your mother when I found it had long entries involving your Allahabad relatives. Of course, the pages that were about me, I tore off carefully and had them bound—in burgundy morocco leather. And yes, I still have the letters I once wrote to Dadu, besides the tin suitcase. You know, initially, I had thought I would return the suitcase too, but Dadu had etched the words "For Sudipto" on it. I took that to mean he wanted me to keep it.'

'Sudipto, after all these years, do you think I'm counting inventory? I am not seeking any explanation for anything,' Mrinalini smiled a somewhat sad smile.

'Then?'

'Well,' she gathered herself with a sigh, 'we discovered something interesting in the diary. It was there right at the beginning, in the first few pages that had got stuck to the diary's molten cover. We could get about three-fourths of it restored. The story has a strange title: "Dream" with a question mark.'

'Really! How did you manage to salvage that? And what is "Dream" about? Have you brought it with you?' I was quite curious.

'A friend of Gunjan has her father in the forensic department. This gentleman, Mr Dhoorjati Sanyal, helped us out. Gunjan got copies of the deciphered script made. And yes, we've brought a copy for you,' Mrinalini said, and after a pause added, 'It's a strange account. You with your ESP and Jung may be able to make something out of it.'

Gunjan went in and brought me the copy.

I would not wait and fumbled for an excuse to get to my room upstairs. 'My ESP says I should read it alone,' I told the mother-daughter duo, bounding up the wooden stairs, oblivious of my 'rattling knee'.

~

Dream?

—*Dwarakanath Chatterjee*
Jhargram

Shibu's little one Dina puts me into a tizzy. The tiny chap has this uncanny habit of popping questions that make a mockery of my years, my so-called learning and my supposed accomplishments. 'Dadu do you have to wear your glasses to see dreams?' the five-year-old asked me today, sitting on my knees with his legs dangling when I told him I had had a strange dream last night.

'Then how do you see?' He was surprised when I told him no.

Dina's wonder rakes up from the bushels of memory, a similar poser my neighbour Chamrette had placed before me years back. That would have been just a couple of months before he was felled by the stray poisoned arrow in his mango orchard.

Chamrette had just finished reading a book by some American psychiatrist and when he dropped in the day after, sporting his trademark pith hat, khakis and canvas shoes, he was full of it. Especially, of the strange incident of an elderly lady, who having been reclaimed from coma following an insulin shock, told the attending emergency doctor she had seen him rush into her cabin and in the hurry drop his pen, which was now resting at the foot of the dextrose stand nearby. The doctor, stupefied beyond words, had taken some time to react to the message and retrieving the eighteen-carat Cross, left the cabin, shaking his head. The fact that the just resurrected patient was blind, and had been so for several years, had unnerved him.

'Chatterjee, sometimes people do see without eyes. You yourself do that in your dreams. How do you think you do that?' he had asked me, sending me into a tizzy.

And now it must be the little one, taking a dig at my self-assurance all so innocently.

'Dadu why are you keeping quiet? What dream did you see last night?' It's little Dina again, still dangling his legs, licking a cream biscuit and making a mess of it. Completely oblivious of the storm his questions raise within me.

'Let me think baba. Ah yes!

'Dina, I saw a train in my dream last night. And very strangely, when the train whistled, the sound it made was that of a shehnai! And, who do you think got off the train? Mrinalini! She looked so happy. She was wearing jeans, jeans 'pentool', like girls in the cities do nowadays. How smart she looked, like an English lady. And she was carrying a bag that looked like a crocodile.'

'Crocodile!' Dina shouted in excitement.

'Not a real crocodile. A bag that looked like it was made of crocodile skin. And you know what was there in that crocodile bag? A jar of drinking chocolate Mrinalini had bought with her own money. A gift for me! Mrinalini teaches English to school children and makes quite a tidy sum. She will teach you too when she visits me here.

'And yes, there was a young boy with her. A tall lanky fellow with a bushy moustache who was busy looking around, as if making a note of everything. His face seemed to have a smile pasted on it. But every now and then he would peer at his wristwatch and grow sad as he put it to his ear. It seemed to me he did not like the tick-tock, the sound of time ticking by. Otherwise, the boy appeared easy going and friendly. Not like the city-bred boys nowadays. And he had a rucksack, something like a school bag, on his shoulders I think.'

'Made of crocodile?'

'No baba, an ordinary bag... Then all of a sudden Chamrette appeared, holding his pith hat in his hands—his feet were bare. Chamrette too had noticed the young man with Mrinalini. "A failed poet," he commented, "looking for refuge in a biography: yours and his own." I protested, saying he was talking through his hat, and moreover, we were yet to know anything about the young man. In fact, we did not even know who he was. But Chamrette would not take back his comment. "Chatterjee, learn to look with your eyes closed," was all he would say.

'I closed my eyes and it was then that the tune of the shehnai hit me. It was a doleful tune—filled me with grief. And I saw a gloomy cottage sitting atop dark mountains. The sky was strangely overcast. I asked Chamrette why the hell the wretched tune was being played. "Ask the young man," Chamrette said, and I walked up to the boy and put the question forth. He kept staring at me with sorrowful eyes, stroking his strangely purple neck all the while. After a long time he sighed and in a broken voice said, "I don't know. Ask Mrinalini." But Mrinalini would not say anything. When I insisted, she smiled through her tears and said she had no answer. Chamrette nodded, saying our sweetest songs are those that tell of the saddest thoughts.'

'I cannot understand anything Dadu,' little Dina protested. 'Your story is rotten.'

Then his face lit up: 'Dadu, didn't you see red butterflies in your dream? Dragonflies with long long tails? Big brown centipedes? Shall I tell you a secret, Dadu? When these centipedes grow up they become big rumbling trains blowing smoke from the holes in their heads and they go *koooo jhakajhain jhakajhain!*'

What a child!

Dina slipped off my knees and ran off towards the staff quarters, saying, 'I'm going to Maa.'

I called after him, but he would not return.

I sank back into my chair and last night's dream swamped my thoughts again.

[*Beyond this line the text could not be deciphered, except for a few stray words such as 'sun', 'jacaranda', 'Saraswati', 'blood', 'mahogany', and 'Mrinalini', besides some prepositions and articles. There appear to have been around seven paragraphs after this and going by the word density, these paras would together have had a little over 1,000 words.—DS*]

~

'Sir, Madam calling down. Dinner ready,' the manservant who had opened the door upon my arrival at The Retreat, startled me.

'Dinner is always ready,' I mumbled absent-mindedly, my mind still dwelling on Dadu's dream.

I followed the man downstairs mechanically and was about to get into the kitchen after him when he stopped astonished and showed me the way to the dining room.

I stood still on the spot for some time, and then decided to go out into the open.

The sky had cleared. I looked up at the inky blue canvas through the filigree of leaves and found Kaalpurush peering down at me. Just as it used to in Jhargram. An owl screeched somewhere, and jackals howled from recollection.

'Cigarette?' an old familiar voice asked.

I turned around. But there was no one.

And then, all of a sudden, without notice or warning, the dam within burst.

I groped for the railing at the edge of the lawn even as the deluge threatened to breach the embankments of my eyes. The past came swirling back, in oceanic waves, with the salt probing for the secret wounds of memory. Lightning struck from the blue, turning the panorama of undulating silhouettes of Pangot into the red winding forest path that had once led to Dadu's bungalow at Jhargram.

I closed my eyes. Ages had gone by since I had steeled my heart to the onslaughts of capricious fantasy: a lime-washed bungalow shimmering amidst lush verdant dappled-sunlight greens; the lingering caress of the forest breeze and of familial touch; hushed cheers and laughter between leaves at the wobble of toddling feet; the fading light of a melting sun making way for the fragrant embrace of an amorous night...

Aeons would have passed by the time I was able to drag my mind back to the barren rocky landscape of the present from the chimerical land of fruitless possibilities.

'I'm all right, I'm all right,' I kept telling myself, 'I can go in now.'

And as I turned to get into the cottage, there was Mrinalini leaning against the entrance, clutching at the volume of Neruda, staring at me through her tears.

'*Love is brief,*' she whispered, '*forgetting lasts so long...*'

The Portrait of an Artist

It had taken some effort to bury the smouldering embers of Pangot under the ashes of my routine lecturing career. But the respite proved ephemeral. I soon discovered to my great discomfiture that ABCD had all of a sudden decided to take a keener interest in my career. Apparently, the feedback he had received from students of the journalism course moving into their second year had sent him into deep thought. The outcome of which was the unexpected opinion that I would perhaps have made a brilliant professor, were it not for certain serious shortcomings: a lazy disposition, an introverted nature, and the absence of a PhD on my CV. Each of the three factors, according to the unduly concerned principal, was potent enough to wreck an academic's prospects single-handedly.

Calling me into his office one day, ABCD said he could do very little about the first two factors since they were deeply-embedded character traits and seeking to change someone's nature was as futile as trying to straighten a mongrel's tail. But the third shortcoming, the lack of a PhD, could be remedied. Towards that end, the considerate person that he was and in exercise of his powers as the final authority of the private college, he had decided to restrict my role as a lecturer, giving me only journalism classes to the exclusion of English literature classes. The time thus freed I was to devote to working on my doctoral thesis, which would be supervised by his one-time college rival Prof EFGH (actually, I have forgotten the name), who now headed the department of journalism at the Calcutta University.

I protested. Going to the extent of saying that, as correctly observed, the first two factors were so dominant, the third would always hold true: I would never have a PhD on my CV.

'There is a fourth factor,' ABCD told me sarcastically. And when I did not ask him what that was, he grew agitated. 'At least you should want to know what it is!'

'All right sir, tell me,' I climbed down.

'You are too adamant and argumentative. Like my wife. She just would not take the intravenous drips and the injections. And she paid for that with her life. She was stupid.' He stared at my face for some time scanning it for reactions, then lunged to deliver the knockout punch. 'I've heard some students of English Honours call you Stupido in private. But I tell you, it's all your own fault. You have only yourself to blame for that.'

I would not swallow the bait. 'I'm sorry to hear about your wife sir,' I said, and asked, 'What was she suffering from?'

ABCD looked surprised, and gradually a cloud came over his face. Getting back into his chair, he said, 'I lost my wife within two years of our marriage. She died of Asiatic cholera.'

'Love in the time of cholera!' I sighed within, thinking the encounter had ended. But it had not. ABCD, after remaining silent for a while, suddenly thrust a question at me. 'Are you married?'

'Well, since you insist, yes and no. I got married once, but live alone now.'

'Why?' he asked, but thankfully, was quick to realize he was being too inquisitive. Changing strategy, he counselled, 'Sudipto, I strongly suggest you take a week off. Go on a holiday. Give this PhD thing a good long thought. It will help you in your career.

Come back after a week and tell me what you have decided. You may go now.'

I had got up to leave, when the gentleman, still unable to come out of the counsellor's role, suggested I visit Netarhat, near Ranchi, where he had once spent a week in springtime with his wife. 'When she was alive,' he added, and I put on a suitably enlightened look.

Eventually, I was persuaded to consider the principal's suggestion seriously, the only remaining hitch being the necessity of having to spend at least two days with my parents at Ranchi, one on the way to Netarhat and the other on the return journey. There would be too many questions, regrets and suggestions—so distressed were they about my marital misfortune—and I wanted no recap of the Sraboni episode; the soap itself I had grown weary of. But providence arranged to remove this niggle too. Ironically, a letter from my mother arrived in the nick of time to inform me the Ranchi household had made reservations to travel lock, stock and barrel over the following week to Puri in Orissa. To persuade the Holy Triad of Jagannath, Balabhadra and Subhadra at (the priest-infested) Sri Jagannath Temple into casting a more benign look at me, besides at a clutch of relatives who too were going through some rough patch or the other. I finalized my Netarhat plans immediately, fearing the premature Trinitarian blessings pouring in would run dry any moment.

I took the South Eastern Railway's Howrah-Hatia Express, on which I had been a regular traveller in a bygone era, from Calcutta to Ranchi, passing en route a small railway station silhouetted by ancient sal, mahogany, mehul and neem—Jhargram—at which my heart sought to alight, pointing at the futility of the parallel steel tracks stretching vainly into the gloom that the railway halogens failed to dispel. Memories, 'misty water-coloured memories', tugged at something within. But the head prevailed.

Getting off at the Ranchi railway station early next morning I straightaway took a rickshaw to the State Bus Depot in the vicinity, intending to catch a bus to Netarhat, the first one available. But luck proved elusive. Buses there were quite a few, but all seats had been booked for the day. I would have to wait till the next morning.

I got a front window-seat reserved in the next day's 6.30 a.m. bus to Netarhat and checked into the BNR Hotel, a sprawling British-era public house once frequented by officials of the erstwhile The Bengal Nagpur Railway Company. I was put up in the old wing, in an immense room with scanty furniture and an air conditioner that found the soaring summer temperature a bit too hot to handle.

The next morning, I checked out of BNR after an early breakfast and landed at the bus depot, where an idling bus, just washed and garlanded with fresh marigolds, stood ready for its hundred and fifty-odd kilometre uphill journey into the soothing cools of Netarhat, the queen of Chhotanagpur nestling amidst virgin forests and green hillocks well over 3,000 feet above sea level.

The journey, unlike my regular commuting in an overcrowded city bus—2B or not 2B—was quite refreshing. And as the State-run luxury bus wound its way up over the pebble-strewn road, the view from the window kept changing. First, it was the broad leaves of the mahogany and flocks of garrulous alexandrine parakeets that caught my fancy. Then, as the bus gained height, I could not take my eyes off the tall pine trees, rising from among colourful whorls of poinsettia, marigold, and wild rose to reach out to the blue skies above.

But as the bus took the final turn to Netarhat, I knew I was in trouble. The whole place was swarming with summer tourists of various shapes, sizes and colours. There were young people in garish clothes, old ones in traditional dhoti-kurtas, bewitched foreigners, and regular tourists sporting baggy shorts and eager looks. The caretaker at the Forest Bungalow, which offered a panoramic view of a green marigold-spotted valley against the backdrop of distant blue hills, told me courteously but quite firmly there was no vacancy and I would best return to Ranchi by the four o'clock bus. The two or three private hotels nearby were all overbooked, and there was no possibility of my finding a room anywhere. I pleaded with him, told him I was coming all the way from distant Calcutta, but the wiry old man would not listen. Finally, a generous tip and a sealed 750 ml bottle of whisky, bilayti as he called it, did the trick. Hariah, the caretaker, finally said I could be accommodated, provided I was willing to share a room with another guest.

Reluctantly, I followed Hariah into an enormous room with bay windows and a fireplace. There were two beds on either side. The one that faced the wall would have to be mine. Hariah said the other guest was out for a walk in the nearby village and would be back for his late lunch soon. But it had hardly been an hour when the bona fide occupant walked in, reeking of country liquor. Tall, emaciated and rather shabbily dressed, the man stared at me for sometime while stroking his unkempt salt-and-pepper beard, and finally introduced himself as 'I'm no Van Gogh, but I'm an artist still'. Then, quite abruptly, he turned around and went to his corner to gaze out of the window at the narrow cobbled path leading to the bungalow gate, leaving me to withdraw my foolishly extended hand into my pocket.

Not knowing how to react to the gaunt, staccato artist who appeared to resemble someone I knew but could not place, I approached Hariah in the kitchen. The caretaker-cum-cook said the artist had entered his name and address illegibly in the guest register, but was a harmless man though not entirely normal and almost always drunk; he was given to sobbing loudly in his dreams and walking in his sleep once in a while, but when he painted he would have a smile on his face. Further, he had been occupying the room for the past one month with no signs of departing. Apparently, he had come to Ranchi for some treatment and on the doctor's advice decided to stay put at Netarhat as long as the summer lasted. Also, he had some influential relative in the nearby town, some sort of a don, who paid his bills and had his room booking extended periodically.

'How old would he be?' I asked Hariah, and was enlightened with 'somewhere between forty and sixty'. It was pointless quizzing the caretaker further, and skipping lunch I decided to explore the surroundings instead. I remembered a friend having told me there was a small lake a short walk from the Forest Bungalow, concealed by the surrounding greenery, and that this spot had been taken off tourist guides ever since a villager had been found dead there, mauled by a bear and strangled by a python—an unlikely double whammy that had perhaps been cooked up to keep the waters clean.

Trudging along the narrow hilly path leading away from the forest bungalow I wandered among unfamiliar trees and wild conifers whistling in the breeze beneath a cobalt sky till I reached the promised lake. It was a magnificent sight. There were no tourists around, and I sat on the bank watching the ripples emerge and spread out continually towards the opposite end. There was a small windmill on the side where the ripples journeyed, and a small boat tethered to a post on the edge, pitching in the tiny waves of the wind-spurred lake.

Time passed by on tiptoes, until, all of a sudden, a magic wand turned the lake into the ancient holy river at Babughat, its small waves reflecting the golden rays of the setting sun on their tiny crests, and its vast gleaming expanse dotted at places by far-off steamers, lugubrious in their anticipation of the impending evening, and one among them carrying a lonesome girl, on her way back home from the university, seated on a wooden plank, leaning against the railing, her chin on her palm, staring into the distance, but looking within. An era sailed away, leaving the soft river breeze to gently fan those golden embers seeking vainly to come to life in the golden waters.

A pine cone splashed into the lake, dragging the mind back to the present: the tranquillity of the surrounding forest, the gently pitching boat in the distance, the languid blades of the picture book windmill, the undulating landscape and the winding hilly road, lined by whispering pines. The clear light by now had given way to a crimson glow and I got up reluctantly to return to the bungalow and my shabby roommate.

Back in the room, I found the artist poring over a large painting. Looking closer I realized he was weeping, the tears streaming down his cheeks to be lost somewhere in the tangled overgrowth. Feeling rather awkward, I was about to go out when he called me. 'Look at this,' he pleaded in a broken voice pointing to the painting before him. I had to turn back. The canvas was certainly extraordinary, though smudged in places. Blue rolling hills formed the backdrop to a deep green valley spotted with golden flowers and at the centre was a woman, strangely familiar, with a pitcher on her head. With one hand she was balancing the pitcher and with the other trying to hold down her flowing skirt billowing in the wind.

As I looked closer, the artist said the woman—Emma as he called her—had only disguised herself as a milkmaid and it was just a matter of time, days in fact, before he would be calling the bluff. He knew Emma had been following him, through town and country, over several years, but she would not come to him till he was clean, completely clean—cleansed by the seven tongues of Agni.

'Cleansed of what?' I asked, unable to make any sense of the babble.

'Oh, of the sins I have committed.'

'What sins?' I was a bit concerned now, not knowing what next the man would come up with.

The artist mulled over the question for some time and suddenly turned hostile.

'Why should I tell you?' his voice was rough.

'It's you who talked of sins. I never asked you!'

The artist chose to sulk for a while, and then turned to me as if we were friends.

'What do you think of Emma?'

'She's beautiful,' I looked again at the lovely face that had evidently been painted with great care.

'Of course she is! She looks especially pretty in these surroundings, you know. I never saw her in a skirt before.'

'Where did you meet her?'

'The first time you mean? I don't know. Actually, I've forgotten, to be honest. You see, I've been meeting her and losing her over so many lives, through so many countries, centuries...'

'In this life?' I would not let him take off again.

'Where else, but in the abode of the Pandavas?'

'I see. But she has an English name. Not very Indian, I mean. She looks Indian though.'

'What's in a name! What is your name, by the way?' the artist looked up from the painting.

'Sudipto Banerjee. And you are?'

'That bloody "jee" again!' he muttered, visibly ruffled. 'Oh, I would never have allowed Hariah to put you up in my room had I known you are a jee,' he continued, raising his voice. 'All jees are heartless, cruel. Bloody brahmins, full of curses. You read the Mahabharat, Ramayan, and you'll find all the sages, the brahmins, cursing someone or the other all the time.'

'You have a point,' I said, eager to end the conversation.

But the artist would not let go of me. 'For aeons have I roamed the roads of the earth, from the seas of Ceylon to the shores of Malay,' he began reciting from *Banalata Sen*, but bungled as he improvised, 'To be with Emma, to be by her side, in good times and bad.'

I did not know what to say and was beginning to feel quite uneasy, when Hariah, to my immense relief, knocked and walked in. He wanted to know if we would have our dinner at the dining hall or in the room. 'Dining hall!' I cried out, keen not to engage with the artist in a private conversation over dinner. The artist said he wanted no meal.

I was about to proceed to the dining hall when the artist suddenly declared, 'You know, I have just a few months to live.'

I stopped in my tracks.

'Why? What is it that you suffer from?' I asked, wondering if it was something contagious.

'You see, once Emma troubled me so much that I drank poison. But I did not die. I was in a hospital for a long time, and when I was released the doctor asked me to give up alcohol and get myself checked every month. Initially I did that, then stopped. When I went to Ranchi this time, my brother took me to a doctor, who said I have no more than a few months left. Apparently, everything inside has rotted. I'm finished. If only I could see Emma once before I die,' he covered his face with his thin hands.

Though ill at ease, I could not help pitying the man. And in a moment of weakness said I would make a sincere attempt at looking for his Emma and requesting her, on his behalf, to visit him if he gave me her telephone number or address.

The artist wept bitterly.

At length, pulling himself together, he said, 'Do you think she will listen to you? She's cruel. Very cruel indeed. She kicked me out of her house. She and her fat mother. Over some trifle. My little child watched with horror...'

'Who is this Emma?' I asked with alarm, a chill running down my spine.

'Actually, Emma is not her real name. I call her Emma. Her initials are MM. I turned that into Emma... What happened? Wait, come back...please...take down her address...'

Ringed and Buttoned Up

My frenzied rush from Netarhat to Ranchi and then from Ranchi to Calcutta, a hysterical journey with hills, valleys and plains blurring past unseeing eyes, appears all too foolish now. Much like the panicked dash of the Baghdad merchant's servant to Samarra to unwittingly honour his appointment with Death in the chilling parable, *The Appointment in Samarra*.

But the desperation to get out of Netarhat had been genuine then.

The artist's account had shaken me up so badly that I rushed out of the Forest Bungalow instantly and spent the night in the open at the place where the bus had dropped me earlier in the day. An eternity later, with the sun having risen a good few metres above the distant hills, a bus arrived, already packed with people and ready to fall apart, but still willing to squeeze in more on its routine lurch towards Ranchi.

Getting off at Ranchi, I went directly to the station and queued up at a ticket counter seeking to have my reservation advanced to the current evening. But the berths in all classes were fully booked, and all I was given in exchange for a confirmed, albeit the next day's, booking was some small currency and an ordinary ticket that promised me entry into the unreserved compartment and nothing besides. I spent an hour or two in the waiting room, and when evicted from there, sat under a large peepul tree, eating salted peanuts and rusks, watching helplessly the tormenting images from the previous night take turns to well up from the bottom of a gingerly-held earthen tea cup and appear on the shimmering surface, one after the other, my desperate attempts to scatter them with a gusty puff utterly futile.

Eventually, as night fell and the neons at the station blinked into luminescence, the Howrah-Hatia Express rumbled in, sending all those with ordinary tickets, and those without, into a mad scramble. I got swept by the crowd rushing towards the two unreserved compartments and soon found myself within, but unable to make it to any seat, my suitcase having failed to squeeze through the mass of unyielding flesh. I had no choice but to station myself near the two stinking lavatories and spent the night seated on the suitcase, leaning against a metal panel on which some frantic lover had etched his bleeding heart pierced by an undersized arrow.

From Howrah to Ballygunge Phari the next morning was a bumpy ride in an ancient black-and-yellow Ambassador, the usual streets, the familiar buildings and the accustomed squalor painting a liniment over my frayed nerves. And the moment my apartment complex, Anandalok, zoomed into view I heaved a sigh of relief, looking forward to a mute and uncomplaining sleep—one not poisoned by memories, dreams or reflections.

But as I unlocked the main door and stepped in, my eyes fell on two envelopes that had been slipped in. Both looked ominous. The first, I noticed, had 'Om Ganga' printed diagonally on its upper left corner, which meant someone I knew had passed away, while the other featured a familiar scrawl. Both had been hand-delivered; they bore no postage stamp. I set my suitcase down and picked up the envelopes. The first one contained an invitation to a prayer meeting for the departed soul of the late Smt

Kamalini Mukherjee, Mrinalini's mother. The second enclosed the survivor's note saying I had been missed at the prayer meeting and should make it convenient to visit Shyambazar at the earliest; the matter was urgent. The last word was underlined.

The servant of the Baghdad merchant had been outwitted and outmanoeuvred twice over. I hit the street again, trying to flag down a taxi that would take me to Shyambazar. And in about forty minutes I was at the doorstep of Mrinalini's ancestral house, unwashed, unrested and a trifle uncomfortable over my inability to condole the death of a person who, all said and done, had never harmed me. As the doorbell rang, hysterical as ever, I realized I was a bit apprehensive too. The same boy servant, now taller and somewhat impassive, ushered me into a large sitting room.

Mrinalini came in within seconds, pale and dishevelled. Grief was written all over her face, and it was clear she had reduced considerably since our last meeting at Pangot. She looked defeated, and I could not help feeling sorry for her. Getting up I waited for her to take her seat and then sat down at the other end of the three-seater. For a while Mrinalini seemed to struggle within, but could not hold back her tears and broke into sobs. Covering her face with her hands, she kept saying she had been cruel—cruel all along, cruel to everyone who had come into her life. I could only watch, not knowing what emotions brought about this admission of guilt even as the words of the emaciated artist—the discarded husband of MM—returned to haunt me afresh.

At length, Mrinalini composed herself. 'I must confess Sudipto, the story of my cruelty begins with you. You are my first victim,' she said, looking away and extending her hand towards me. I almost recoiled.

'Oh, come on!' I tried to sound casual as I watched the retreating hand from the corners of my eyes.

'No, don't say that. I know how much I made you suffer,' she now turned to face me. 'People might say it was just a college romance. But I know it was not just that... You will not believe this, but even after I had fallen for Bhanu, I hated the idea of you ever getting married. So selfish was I. And I could never stand Sraboni. Even after I was married, settled and pregnant with Gunjan!' Her tears flowed freely.

I willed myself into sitting still, making sure my face revealed nothing.

Eventually, drying her eyes with the end of her sari, Mrinalini asked me to wait a moment and left the room.

'The reason why I asked you to come here,' she said, holding out a fairly large jewellery box.

I was perplexed. 'What is this? And why?'

'Open it. It's from my mother.'

'What!'

Unlocking the intricately designed silver box, I found in it a set of diamond-studded gold kurta buttons and a heavy gold ring with a diamond solitaire. There was a small note pinned to the red satin lining under the lid.

Dear Sudipto, these too Baba had left for you. I had held them back thinking the occasion would soon arise when I could make a gift of the buttons and the ring to you on his behalf. But it seems I will not live that long. God bless you.—KM

A gift, Dadu's gift, withheld for long and then suddenly delivered—for what? I looked up but found no answer in the pallid face of Mrinalini, whose resemblance to her mother from the angle appeared extraordinary even in that moment of bewilderment. But it did not take long for the puzzle to unravel itself. I slumped into the sofa, holding the silver box in my awkward hands, tormented afresh by the token of Dadu's love and by what it betokened.

Fighting a battle with the barrage of emotions threatening to come over ground, I kept the box on the centre table.

'I cannot accept this,' I tried keeping my voice level. 'I know I'm going against the wishes of two dead persons, one among whom I had loved no less than you,' I added, regretting immediately the unnecessary comparison.

But Mrinalini did not react. She kept staring at the table and finally sighed, 'I had my right to force anything on you forfeited long back. Do as you wish.'

The awkwardness of the situation was increasing by the second, and I knew I had to get away before things spun out of control. Mumbling something about several chores pending at home, I got up to leave. Mrinalini smiled a weak smile and said Ram Singh would drop me home.

'No, no, no. No need for that,' I tried to hurry out lest I be trumped once again.

A blinding pain shot through my leg. I crashed like a log, my head hitting the armrest of the sofa as I fell.

English Patient

The drive to the hospital was excruciating. Every time Ram Singh hit a pothole or rumbled over tram tracks the pain was unbearable and I felt like throwing up. Mrinalini held my hand and kept up a chatter probably to make sure I did not pass out. Gunjan sat beside the driver, her dilated eyes staring at us from the rear view mirror. We screeched in at the Emergency, and I was wheeled into a large room in which the sight of several patients in various stages of morbidity, lying attached to tubes and gadgets, only added to my anxiety. A doctor came in, took a long look at my knee and poked here and there as I bit into my lip. A nurse put me on intravenous drip.

'How did the dislocation happen Mrs Mukherjee?' the doctor asked.

'He was hurrying and his knee caught the edge of the table.'

'Closed reduction is out of the question,' he said, nodding his head.

Mrinalini said she did not get him at which he coolly said, 'Surgery. It's a recurrent case, I'm certain of that. Must have happened earlier too. But the musculature is intact. Three weeks in the hospital, some weeks of physiotherapy, and he should be ready to play football!'

'And he had hit his head against the chair...is that serious?' Mrinalini sounded nervous.

The doctor produced a torch from nowhere and flashed it in my eyes.

'Did he pass out? Did he bleed from the ears? Did he throw up, Mrs Mukherjee?'

'No, he has been conscious all along. And no, no bleeding from the ears. But there was some nausea.'

The doctor took out a pen and ran the tip along the sole of my left foot from the heel to the toes and as the foot twitched, he smiled. 'No head injury,' he declared, and looking at me said, 'You won't know when the surgery happens. Just relax.'

'Now please wait outside, madam,' the nurse almost scolded Mrinalini, who would not budge. The doctor intervened, saying, 'Not to worry, Mrs Mukherjee. We'll keep you posted at every step. He's out of pain now.' And turning towards me, he smiled, 'Isn't that so, Mr Mukherjee?'

Woozy though I was, the name jarred, but I was in no condition to seek a corrigendum. Already, gentle waves of sleep were washing over me. The pain had disappeared and in that state of half-wakefulness, many faces, wearing various expressions, took turns to switch into appearance against the backdrop of the white ceiling only to fade as they trailed away into the far corner. The only ones I still remember are that of Shibuda, the awkward epithet 'jamata' on his lips, and of Ghosh Jethu, peering at me from behind the veil of that trademark half-smile.

When I came to, I found two almost identical pairs of eyes staring at me. 'Who are you?' I mumbled, and saw tears welling up in what, on a longer look, seemed to be the older pair. That got me worried and I wanted to sit up. It is then that I realized I was in a hospital bed, with my right leg heavily bandaged and my left hand connected to a drip. Mrinalini stood planted beside the drip stand with Gunjan by her side. The events at the Shyambazar house came rushing back and I sank into the bed, feeling caged and hemmed in.

'How are you feeling?' Mrinalini asked, leaning towards me.

I quickly gathered myself. 'All right, nothing to complain about. The surgery was long overdue. I had been unnecessarily apprehensive. It didn't hurt at all, the surgery. The doctor was right. Good it's now done. Can I have some water please? And what time is it?'

'You don't have to talk so much. It's evening. Time to go to bed,' Mrinalini said running her hand over my head and asked Gunjan to go over to the nurses' station and inform the sister on duty that I had come to and wanted water.

The nurse marched in and repeated Mrinalini's question. I said I was feeling fine. She checked the drip and allowed me just two or three sips of water, leaving with the assurance that I would be permitted a glassful in an hour or so.

It was the beginning of a three-week ordeal. I was worried about several things: the hospital bills that would have to be settled, all those who would have to be informed of the accident, the leave application that would have to be sent to the college, arrangements that would have to be made to clean up my apartment at least once a week, the electricity bill that would have to be paid to prevent disconnection—the list was indeed long.

Mrinalini would visit me twice a day, sometimes accompanied by Gunjan, and always bring with her something or the other. In the mornings it was usually flowers and newspapers, and in the evenings it would perhaps be a bar of chocolate, a sweet dish that had been prepared at home, comic books with Gunjan's name written artistically on them, magazines, and so on. At the end of a fortnight or so, I asked her to bring me a notebook and a pen, and a few inland letters besides.

'Who do you want to write to?' she asked.

'That's not very polite,' I said, and Mrinalini appeared embarrassed.

'OK, OK,' she hastened, 'no personal questions.'

I laughed. 'What is there about me that you don't know already?'

'Everything...as if you didn't know!' she said and began laughing too.

'I want to write to the principal of my college applying for fresh leave, and maybe to my parents asking them to come over and take charge of the apartment for some time and make all the payments. And I want to note down my rambling thoughts in the notebook. It's very boring during the day, you know. There's nothing to do, I can't stand the TV, and I've never been a great reader. Maybe I could start writing things.'

'Will you take some good advice?'

'Sure.'

'There's no need to write to anyone, especially your parents at Ranchi. Why get them worried and have them rush to Calcutta? Once you're discharged from hospital and can potter about, just go over, spend some time with them, and give them an account of your stupid accident, with all the gory details. The principal of your college I can speak to on the phone and if required I can see him in his office with all the hospital papers. And as far as the upkeep of your flat is concerned, Ram Singh can make all the payments and get the house cleaned once a week. These are small things, Sudipto. You don't have to break your head over them. Especially in this state.'

'Well, if that sofa in your drawing room couldn't break my head perhaps nothing can,' I joked and we both laughed.

'But do you agree to my suggestions?'

I thought for some time and said yes, adding, 'But there's one thing I must know.' I could see Mrinalini stiffen in her chair.

'What is it?' she asked, knitting her eyebrows.

'How much would the hospital bill come to?'

'Do you have health insurance?'

'No. The one I had expired long back.'

'Several crores then.'

'I'm not joking.'

'That's none of your business,' Mrinalini appeared quite firm.

'Oh no, Mrinalini you have to tell me that.'

'Certain things are not negotiable, you know, and this happens to be one of them.'

'I'm sorry, but I have to say the same thing.'

We kept silent for some time, and then I repeated my question. Mrinalini got up in a huff saying she would leave if I went on nagging.

'Mrinalini, your leaving scares me no more,' the words just slipped out of my lips.

Mrinalini was stunned. And so was I. Never had I spoken to her the way I just did. Not even during our college days, when occasionally we would get into a passionate fight, say, over why I had been so entertaining of some fresher, some pretty girl, from such and such department. I would deny the charge, and my explanation failing to convince her, I would tell Mrinalini to go get herself checked by a shrink.

'I'm sorry, Mrinalini,' I tried to make amends. 'I didn't mean to be rude. I take it back. You don't deserve it. After all that you've done for me during these last few days. I'm really sorry.'

Mrinalini said nothing, refusing to even accept my apologies. She kept standing for some time, looked at her watch, said the visiting hours would soon be over, and left wishing me a routine good night.

That night at the hospital was distressful. The body pinned down to the bed, the mind hobbled over numerous terrains— some recently traversed, some left behind in a bygone era— tripping over some stone here or stepping on some bramble there, and the remembered pain flaring up to bring into sudden illumination faces and events that would all leave, after their brief existence under the purple lights of contused memory, the same bitter feeling: of helplessness, utter helplessness.

Mrinalini did not come to visit me the next morning. Her daughter did. Bringing with her a youthful smile and a bouquet of oriental lilies. I could only watch her flitting about in the room, settling down near my bed for a while and then getting up to perch herself on the window sill at the far end, asking questions and not waiting for answers. She would be a few years older than my own Titir, who, I imagined, would also bloom into a happy maiden some day, having cast off the dark memories of a distant father.

'What's your mom up to?' I asked as the cheerful teenager paused in her chatter.

'She's gone to your college, to see the principal. And get your leave approved.'

'Oh! But she never told me she would be doing that.'

'I see,' was her simple reply.

'So she would be here in the evening?'

'Unlikely.'

'Why?'

'Because you upset her last evening. And also, she'll be taking Ram Singh and a maid to get your apartment cleaned, settle the bills and bring you the mail you would have received in the last few days.'

'She'll go to my apartment! But why? And where would she get the key from?'

'The hospital handed over the key to us and the ring you were wearing when you were taken into the OT. You don't remember that?'

I looked at my hand and could only find a depigmented band at the base of the right middle finger that once sported a blue moonstone mounted on a silver ring, one that my mother had got made for me on the recommendation of some astrologer. This was when I was at Ranchi after the MA examinations, struggling to erase the scar left by the botched suicide attempt.

'But how can she just go there without even asking me? At least...' I checked my outburst, realizing Gunjan would have had nothing to do with her mother's initiatives.

'Please don't be angry,' the child tried to reason with me. 'Mom's doing it all as a friend. What's wrong with that? You went to college together. You know each other for donkey's years. Wouldn't you have done the same if, God forbid, Mom had an accident?'

I kept quiet. And when Gunjan was leaving at the end of the visiting hour, I asked her to tell Mrinalini I would be expecting her in the evening.

But Mrinalini made no appearance in the evening and again it was her daughter filling in for her.

'Mom couldn't come,' Gunjan informed me as she breezed into the room holding out a triangular bar of chocolate. 'She went to your apartment straight from your college. Mom says your apartment was in a bigger mess than my room and she got tired tidying up the place. But your principal was nice and quite concerned. He asked Mom to take good care of you and not take it to heart if you argued unnecessarily with her.'

I could feel the blood shooting up to my head, but kept shut. The very idea of Mrinalini shuffling things around in my den and perhaps even rummaging through my drawers was revolting. If this was not a clear breach of privacy, nothing else would ever be, I wanted to yell, but checked myself. Why take it out on a child? What did she know!

'You know you quite impressed me with your knowledge of trees and plants at Pangot, remember? The way you rattled off the names... What grass was it? Kikuyu, right?' I asked, determined to take my mind away from the break-in and bring up something cheerful.

'Mom claims I've got it from her,' Gunjan smiled.

'But you're not into sports, no?'

'Oh no! Never had a taste for it.'

'No game appeals to you!'

'Only Scrabble, that too, sometimes.'

'Well we'll play Scrabble one of these days then,' I said, but Gunjan did not seem too eager.

Mrinalini came in the next morning, holding a bunch of roses in one hand and a large envelope in the other.

'It seems you've been upset with me?' she smiled as she placed the roses on the bedside table.

'Yes of course!' I said, and told her I should have been informed before she chose to visit my apartment or talk to the principal of my college.

'Oh stop this bickering,' she swept my protest aside as if it were the mere whining of a grumpy schoolboy. 'If a job has to be done, it has to be done, that's all. No use holding discussions over it. And after all these years, I'm sure you did not fear I'd pick up something from your house or embarrass you before your principal.'

'What nonsense! Whoever said that?' I objected. 'You should have informed me in advance—that's all I meant.'

'Sorry, baba, sorry. You want me to hold my ears and stand up on the bench?'

I had to relent. And eventually we both laughed.

'Here are your bills. The hospital bills, I mean. You wanted me to get them for you.'

'Yes of course,' I said and took the receipts out of the envelope. There were more than a dozen. But all it took me was just a few seconds to figure out that the bills would add up to a humongous sum.

'This would be more than six lakhs!' I exclaimed with horror.

'Yes, this hospital is rather expensive.'

'And you've made these payments already?'

'Yes.'

'And the bills for the next few days that I'm here would add up to another six lakhs?'

'No, not that much. The major expenses are over.'

'Mrinalini, I'm destroyed! How on earth shall I pay you back?'

'I never asked you to.'

'Oh come on! How can I live with such a huge burden of debt sitting on my head?'

'You have to figure that out yourself, I guess.'

'But why did you get me into such an expensive hospital?'

'Sudipto, it's the only one I'm familiar with. And it's supposed to have one of the best orthopaedic centres in Asia. Besides, it is also the nearest to my house. You were in great pain, if you remember.'

'But six lakhs!' I couldn't get to terms with the figure. 'Even if I were to sell off all my belongings, I wouldn't be able to raise that kind of money.'

'Sudipto, six lakhs is just a small recompense to make for the pains I have caused you,' Mrinalini said, turning towards the window. 'You came to visit me on my invitation. But if you still insist, you can pay me back in instalments, say, over ten years, twenty years, or whatever you think it would take you.'

The doctor came in, nattily dressed and wearing his practised cheerfulness, wished both of us a 'very good morning' and got into a chat with Mrinalini. 'Mrs Mukherjee, I've been thinking of telling you this, you're beginning to put on weight again! I'm sure you've turned your treadmill into a towel rack,' he told her, to which Mrinalini retorted, 'Doctor, heal thyself. Have you had the time to look up yourself in the mirror? Mrs Bagchi has taken over the kitchen, is it?' They had a good laugh and the doctor turned to me. 'And how's our English patient? Any pain, Professor Banerjee?'

'No, none at all, doctor.'

'Great! Wish the other patients were like you. So, we take off the bandage in the afternoon, you begin walking with a crutch, first a few steps, and then more, and if everything's OK, tomorrow you're discharged. But you'll have to come back for physiotherapy every day at least for the next fifteen days. After that we can space it out and you can do the exercises at home.'

'But does he have to visit the hospital every day?' Mrinalini asked my question.

'Unless you have a physiotherapist at home, madam,' the doctor joked.

'But can't we get someone on call?'

'Oh sure, you can. My junior will give you some numbers.

You have met Dr Sen, no? Oh yes you have. He was the one at the Emergency the day you brought Mr Banerjee in. You'll find him in the OPD. He knows you.'

I was too befuddled to say anything.

'By the way,' the doctor turned back from the door, 'would you be able to organize some help at home, Professor Banerjee? Madam was saying you live all by yourself, and there's no lift to your apartment. I would strongly suggest you stay a few weeks at the 'Mukherjee palace'. You'll need help. And they used to have a very good cook. Or you could even stay here at the hospital for a few more days. It's up to you. I can recommend that.'

I smiled a wry smile, telling myself that no one would perhaps have ever imagined the adage 'beggars can't be choosers' could take such a bizarre twist.

I was discharged from hospital the next day and driven straight to Mrinalini's home. A couple of servants, appearing from nowhere, helped me in and put me up in a room I could instantly recognise as the one in which I had met Dadu for the last time. The details came back sharp and clear. I had rushed from college on the news that he had taken ill and wanted to see me, and on entering the room had found him lying patiently in bed, awaiting, in his words, 'the sunset and evening star' almost with a smile. I also remembered the strange question he had posed to me then, the answer to which still lay in the dark vaults of the future: 'But where does *your* story end?'

Where indeed? I looked around, feeling completely out of place amidst the opulence: the thick silk curtains, the large four-poster, the marble-top bed-side tables with onyx lamps on them, the large chest of drawers in the corner, the leather sofa set with a carved wooden centre table, the row of Burma teak wardrobes covering an entire wall, the air conditioner wafting down waves of cool air from a corner of the high ceiling, the polished brass light fittings, the ornate ceiling fan...

'It should not be the case that you grow so fond of your cage, you begin to despise your wings,' I repeated Ghosh Jethu's words unmindfully, unaware that Mrinalini stood right behind me.

'It's just a few weeks,' she assured me. I turned my head with a start and sank back in the bed leaning against the gleaming headboard.

'You remember,' I said at length, 'Dadu used to say "I never force events; I allow events to force me"? Maybe it's time I started following him.'

'That would be a good beginning,' Mrinalini smiled.

But good beginnings, as I had come to realize, were more like red herrings, and I was besieged by forebodings. Back in the future, in brooding moments of grim fancy, I sometimes liken, with cinematic exaggeration, the lingering weeks at Mrinalini's house to a cheerless fugitive's fateful plod along a desolate road dimly lit by a failing moon, stretching aimlessly ahead only to be lost amidst the undifferentiated gloom of an unknown land spread thick and ominous over the distant horizon; the rustling trees, the occasional curlew, and the truant moon, now lost and now peeping from behind cumulus clusters, perchance bringing up a smile on the face of the hobbling émigré, only to wipe it away the next moment with a sweep of misgivings and anxiety.

The physiotherapist would come in early, and after a painful half an hour or so with the sadistic gentleman, I would be at the mercy of Mrinalini, who had drawn up for me a detailed list of do's and don'ts—the don'ts including all that I loved and the dos almost everything I hated. For instance, tobacco and alcohol, even in small nutritious doses, had been banned, while plastic-coated pills, smelly milk and modern Bangla poetry had to be savoured at various pre-fixed hours during the day. And as if this were not enough, Mrinalini would insist I have salads by the bucketful, my argument that the art of cooking had developed over millennia and the culinary skills of a race bespoke of its status on the scale of evolution failing to make any impression on her.

For the first few days, I accepted the aggressive hospitality with equanimity, but began voicing my protests soon after. And in this, I was aided and abetted by Mrinalini's daughter, who one day declared suo motu at the dinner table that her mother's treatment of her one-time classmate amounted to nothing but plain and simple ragging, and that except for cigarettes, none of my demands were unjustified. But Gunjan went a little overboard.

'You can stop me from having those liqueur chocolates sitting and rotting in the fridge, but how can you stop Uncle from sending Ram out to get a bottle of whisky?' she challenged her mother. 'He is an adult, and he is buying it with his own money,' she added, instantly realizing that the money part had been unnecessary.

'The money is not the issue,' I stepped in quickly, 'although with the kind of debt I owe your mom, I should not be spending a single farthing on anything I can do without.'

Perhaps it was the subject of debt that raised Mrinalini's hackles.

'Sudipto you have already paid me back,' she announced, raising her voice.

'But how is that?'

'Dadu's gift to you, which Maa had held back, would be worth several times your hospital bills. In fact, if you insist on repaying me, I will have no option but to get the things valued and hand over the difference to you,' Mrinalini said, as I looked shocked. Getting up triumphantly from her chair, she now declared, 'Sudipto, there can be no loan between you and me. That's the final word. I will not hear anything more on this.' Her angry gaze next fell on her daughter. 'And Gunjan, I'm quite disappointed with you,' she scowled, 'I thought you knew when to open your silly mouth and when to keep it shut.'

I would have protested, but Mrinalini marched away to her room leaving a hapless Gunjan staring at her unfinished dinner. The poor girl had meant no harm, and the reprimand, I thought, was completely undeserved.

Silence fell at the table and the servants standing in the far corner were suddenly reminded of some pending work that would brook no further delay. As they disappeared somewhere inside, I fumbled for words to comfort Gunjan with.

'You know, I had an uncle, Ghosh Jethu,' I began, 'who once told me I would not be able to do much in life unless I had my RH factor corrected. And Ghosh Jethu was always right.'

Gunjan saw through the ploy but made an attempt to come out of the sulk.

'What was he, a doctor? Sorry, what do they call such doctors? Yes, was he a haematologist?'

'Oh no, not a doctor,' I laughed, 'he was a bureaucrat, an accountant actually. You know, initially, I had made the same guess. I had thought RH stood for the Rhesus factor in blood grouping. Then Ghosh Jethu told me RH stood for Rhinoceros Hide. What he meant was, unless I was able to develop a rhinoceros hide, a thick skin that is, I would always remain vulnerable to harsh words, undeserved criticism and so on. People would simply get under my skin and rob me of peace. So, from that day onwards, I have been trying to develop an RH. And I have had some success, I would say.'

'*Sticks and stones may break my bones, but words will never hurt me,*' Gunjan said and smiled, sending me back in a flash to my small apartment at Ballygunge Phari where I sat before an incensed Sraboni with Titir by her side, the duo unable to come to terms with the moniker Stupido that some students at Bengal Renaissance had coined for me, but the two reacting in totally different ways to the disgrace: the mother seeking to overpower the agents of ignominy, and the child struggling to invoke, instinctively, the strength of the inner self to make the ego invulnerable to abuse.

'My child!' I caught Titir's arm in Gunjan's.

The Rains

Mrinalini left soon after lunch the next day along with Ram Singh and a servant to clean my apartment. I had tried to dissuade her saying there was no need since I would be moving in soon and by then had recuperated enough to take care of a 900 square feet flat by myself, but my protestations were taken no notice of. Her remark that I was now in her hands did nothing to relieve my uneasiness.

Weighed down by apprehensions, I sat by a window in my room, staring at the overcast sky and wondering if deep within those slate-grey vaults, in some innocuous corner, there lay some neglected parchment, limed and rolled up, in which the story of my life had been recorded in an ancient hand, and what this prescient account had to tell beyond the current episodes of hospital and hospitality. A sudden gust of wind scattered my thoughts and then came the rain, thick and fast, leaving me with no option but to hurry up and make a clumsy attempt at latching the windows. Gunjan rushed into my room, asked me to move away and bolted the windows one by one. Turning to me she exclaimed, 'The rains at last! Wish I could go up to the terrace.'

'Why don't we?' I asked, uplifted by her exuberance.

'We?' She cast a queer look at me, an eyebrow raised.

'The stitches around my knee have dissolved and the physiotherapist has said I should now try climbing stairs.'

'Cross your heart?'

'Cross my heart,' I placed a hand on my chest as I had seen children do.

'Great!' Gunjan exulted, whirled around on one heel, and asked if she could carry her portable music player with her. 'Why not!' I said and off we went for our conquest of the two flights of stairs.

The climb was difficult, although my sherpa very patient and encouraging. But once we had reached the summit, Gunjan cut loose. Rushing into the rain, she pirouetted about on the terrace, belting out some English-sounding song and pausing and bending over intermittently to pluck her imagined guitar strings as I stood bemused, watching through rain-laden lashes the revolving patterns of youthful delight against the grim backdrop of a still-overcast sky, split occasionally by the purple veins of blinding light.

The performance went on for some ten minutes or so after which Gunjan, exhausted and panting, slumped on the terrace leaning against the water tank, and asked me if I could do her a favour. The cassette player she had placed at the entrance had to be turned on. 'Sure,' I replied, and limping up to the battery-set switched it to 'Play'. For quite a few seconds nothing happened, which prompted me to limp back and turn the volume to 'Max'. Still, nothing happened and as I fiddled with the player trying to see what was wrong a booming voice suddenly burst forth: 'Buddy, chill chill, just chill…' I stepped back startled and before I knew what was happening, it seemed as if several metal utensils were tumbling down the stairs even as somebody was beating the hide off a drum set.

'Oh my god!' I could not help exclaiming, only to see Gunjan pointing at me and rolling in a pool of rainwater doubled up with laughter.

'The music was great, isn't it, Uncle?' Gunjan asked as we paused on the landing between the two flights of stairs, dripping all over.

'Yeah, I almost had a heart attack!'

A peal of laughter, and then, 'That's the right medicine for you, you know. I mean, you are too serious, like Mom. You've to learn to just chill.'

'Buddy, chill chill, just chill,' I mimicked the unknown singer and Gunjan roared with laughter, pausing only to say perhaps frogs croaked better.

Having climbed down the stairs, I asked Gunjan if her mother liked the song and her jaw dropped. 'Are you crazy! Mom says with this song playing no 'kaak cheel' (crow, kite) would dare sit on our roof.'

I loved the play on 'chill' and suggested we turn the lyrics to 'Buddy, kaak kaak, just kaak'

'Oh nooo,' Gunjan remonstrated, 'that's sick, so sick! What a PJ!'

I told her I had a trunk-load of poor jokes in my possession and perhaps it was because of the PJs that some of my students in college had named me Stupido.

'Stupido? From Sudipto? That's a good one!' Gunjan clapped and went into her room, leaving me to wonder at the diversity of human nature: what to one was a funny anagram, to another was a mortal affront.

Mrinalini came in quite late in the evening, looking happy and chewing betel. Entering my room, she handed me a packet, gift-wrapped and sporting a ribbon bow.

'What's this?' I asked.

'Your shirt size should be XL, no?'

'Yes, but...'

'I went to New Market to get curtains, bed sheets and some household stuff. Found the shirt displayed in a shop window and got it for you. You used to have a similar shirt in college, I remember.'

'But what's the occasion? And you've already brought me enough clothes from my flat.' I made no attempt to hide my discomfort.

'The occasion is, you'll be leaving this house soon! Good riddance to bad garbage, as we used to say once upon a time.'

'Mrinalini, as it is I owe you such a lot of money,' I said, 'and then all this! Why must you go on adding to my burden...'

'Oh shut up!' Mrinalini cut me short. 'There is time enough to do the accounts. And to think of money when someone gifts you something! Shameful! You're getting cheap, Sudipto.'

I kept shut, stung by the charge that I equated gifts with money.

Dinner was served soon after and at the table Gunjan told Mrinalini about her rain dance, my poor parody 'Buddy, kaak kaak, just kaak', and the successful attempt at climbing stairs.

'You climbed stairs!' Mrinalini flashed an angry look at me. I said yes, and further, that I proposed to repeat the exercise the next day so that climbing three floors when I returned to my flat was not an uphill task.

'Gunjan, it must be you who nagged him into climbing stairs. And you know how slippery the terrace gets when it rains. What if he slipped and fell? Have you all decided to drive me mad?' Mrinalini fired one missile after another at the hapless girl as I kept pinching the skin on the back of my hand trying desperately to remind her of the RH story I had narrated to her earlier in the day. Gunjan watched my mime from the corners of her eyes and kept raising an eyebrow asking for another hint. Mrinalini caught her in the act and thundered, 'Are you listening to me?'

I had to barge in and tell Mrinalini of Ghosh Jethu's advice to me on growing a rhino hide—the advantages it held over hypersensitive human skin.

Mrinalini heard out the story, sighed and said that with her daughter and I having decided to team up against her, she would have to watch her step henceforth.

The storm having blown over, dinner was a relaxed affair with each of the three partakers looking very pleased and the youngest one giving me a thumbs-up when her mother was not looking. I left the table smiling and had just got into my room when Mrinalini came in and planted herself on the sofa.

'Actually I'm quite relieved you could climb the stairs, you know,' she said.

'Me too.'

'Maybe you'd be able to join us at Pangot again sometime next year... And maybe you could play badminton once again. I'm sure they have tournaments for seniors too.'

'Yeah! Let's see,' I got a tad too excited. 'And if I can, it's you I would have to thank. My first medal or prize or whatever will be dedicated to you. That's a promise. And I will give up smoking. Upon my word...'

'You remember our third year in college?' Mrinalini's eyes shone. 'That had been a glorious year for you. You won all the three titles: singles, doubles and mixed doubles! And three titles for the third year running. Till then, no one else had ever achieved that. Maybe the record still stands!'

I don't know why but all of a sudden my throat grew tight and I kept staring at the sofa. Gunjan walked in, wondering if it was all right if she joined us. And while her mother pondered whether or not to agree, I cleared my throat and said 'Yes, of course'.

'Even our HOD was impressed, remember?' Mrinalini resumed her reminiscence. 'Jawahar Sen, what a scary man he was! You remember that dressing-down you got in public when he warned you against skipping lectures? Oh, I still can't get over that!'

'Who can!' I said.

'What was it about? Tell me...' Gunjan nagged her mother.

'Oh, our HOD JS was yelling at Sudipto with almost the entire department around. He was warning Sudipto that if he went on bunking classes, JS would ensure he was disqualified from taking his BA exams. And your Sudipto Uncle, red in the ears and staring at his own feet, was mumbling "Yes sir, yes sir". Now JS, who was a bit hard of hearing, thought Sudipto was saying "Esther, Esther", trying to suggest it was some girl who held him back from attending classes. "WHO is this Esther?" JS's bellowed, and Sudipto in his nervousness stammered, "The queen, sir, Jewish or Persian, there's some controversy..." At that, JS' eyes almost popped out, and he scurried back to the teachers' room muttering he wouldn't be surprised if Sudipto went about biting people next!'

The three of us were rolling on the sofa.

'And you remember the quiz the seniors made all freshers take on the first day of college?' I asked when we had caught our breath.

'Of course! And the one common question across batches was, "Name the professor at Presidency College who shares with a past Soviet dictator his initials, his temperament and his view that 'one death is a tragedy, one million a statistic'." If any fresher answered "Jawahar Sen", the entire batch would be treated to tea and vegetable chops at Pramodda's canteen.'

'But all said and done, JS had declared a half-day off when I won the badminton championship in the third year, madam. I remain grateful to him for that,' I said, remembering the celebration across batches over the surprise announcement.

'And Gunjan, you know how JS prefaced the announcement?' Mrinalini stood up, and imitating the way JS would scratch his shiny top, look sideways and blink repeatedly before making a speech, announced in a gruff voice: 'Apparently, our boy with those whiskers has won some shuttlecock competition for a record third time; they say it's a "triple hat-trick", whatever that is supposed to mean. You can all go and watch him and other sports fanatics take prizes from our principal at the auditorium this afternoon. There will be no classes after lunch.'

Gunjan clapped and high-fived her mother.

I was back onto the badminton court once again, at the balding patch of green that the main college building enclosed, battling it out with a former junior State champion from the history department as intermittent outbursts of 'Come on!' from along the flanks of the chalk-marked rectangle egged us on. And then, at 14-0, a toss sailing deep onto my backhand and I rushing into the left corner, stationing myself behind the baseline, and covering my backhand, sending the bird back on a diagonal path with a late turn of the oval head into the future historian's territory, and the feather, catching the glint of a thin crepuscular beam to hover ever so briefly over the white tape, dropping delicately onto the other side of the net, to mark the end of a game, a match and a dream; the first two in love, and the last in agony. For a slip from the footboard of a moving tram the same evening would, by dislocating my right knee, dash forever all dreams of a spectacular sporting career.

'Sudipto, can't you move in and stay with us?' Mrinalini's abrupt poser jolted me out of my souring reverie.

I could only gape at her. 'Don't be silly,' I managed eventually.

'But why not?' Mrinalini demanded, as Gunjan excused herself saying she had to finish some homework.

'Mrinalini, we are both married, although we don't live with our spouses. Staying here would look extremely odd. What would your relatives say? You are a woman, and you have a daughter to bring up and marry off.'

'So?'

'What do you mean "so"?'

'Then should I move into your apartment?'

'That would be scandalous!'

'Do you still harbour hopes of Sraboni returning to you?'

'That's not the point.'

'Then what is?'

'It's just not done,' I said, desperately looking for some clinching argument.

'But why? Why is it that the skies would fall if I stayed with you in your apartment? Have the skies fallen since you've been here?'

The encounter with the emaciated artist at Netarhat popped up suddenly and rushed to my defence. 'Mrinalini, it might distress you, but I met your husband at Netarhat sometime back. He is dying and he still misses you and Gunjan,' I said.

For once Mrinalini was stunned and kept quiet for a long time even as I tried frantically to get away from the pile of memories that my hasty trip to Netarhat had left me with.

'My *former* husband—you missed the qualifier,' Mrinalini's voice was icy. 'And what do you know about Mister Bhanu Pratap Sinha whom you *think* you met recently?'

'Not much beyond the fact that you knew him from your JNU days. And that you married him in haste and discarded him likewise.' I had to choose my words with care.

'Yes I met him at JNU. There you're right. But what do you know of him? You probably know he was dismissed from Wanderlust when his school and college certificates were found to have been forged, but what you don't know is that he was also an alcoholic and a racketeer. Bhanu was part of a group that took a cut for almost every contract the hotel gave out to suppliers: from florists to upholsterers to F&B suppliers to newspaper vendors, to everything. It was a big chain. The hotel management had smelt something fishy for long, but did not have the evidence. Finally, the scamsters were nailed down in a sting. Everything was caught on camera. I saw the footage myself. The entire group was asked to put in their papers.'

'Oh!'

'Sudipto, I admit I made a mistake, a terrible mistake, giving you up for Bhanu. I still don't know what it was about him that had swept me off my feet. Maybe, because he came across as a real person; yes, *real*—tangibly, physically, real. And he was so much in love with me—me as a person, as a woman... It was not just the idea of love, some teenage idyllic romance, holding hands and whispering in the ear... He was a man; a man among boys... And he had such a happy disposition, your troubles simply vanished in his presence...used to paint so well... Who would imagine that behind such an exterior there was a criminal lurking all the time! Maybe it was my property he had his eyes on. And Sudipto, remember, I was little more than a teenager then—a girl who had grown up in a broken family, craving protection more than companionship, a girl eager to realize her womanhood... It was a folly, yes a terrible one, but some are destined to learn the hard way...I am sorry that in growing up I ruined your life.'

I remained silent.

'Sudipto, will you never forgive me for marrying Bhanu?' Mrinalini turned her gaze towards me, seeking an immediate answer.

I hesitated, but eventually decided to come out with what I had to say. 'Gandhiji once said forgiveness is the attribute of the strong. I don't know if I'm that strong.'

'Don't say that! Please! Can you not let the past be past? Can you not wake up and see for yourself the nightmare is over? Gone?'

'Mrinalini, the nightmare did not happen in sleep. It happened with the whole world awake...with all the lights on, the shehnai playing and the crowd milling around you and your manly consort, showering you with rose petals and expensive gifts. I had been coerced into attending the wedding, to show the world that there remained nothing between the two of us...

'I still remember how hesitant you were about taking the cellophane-wrapped *Banalata Sen* from my hands. As if the gift itself would blight your conjugal bliss! Or was it that the gift was too small, too cheap for the occasion? Mrinalini, a book was all I could afford at that time... I was still unemployed, remember? Living off my poor father, undergoing counselling in Calcutta after that miserable attempt at ending my life.'

'Oh stop, stop it!' Mrinalini broke down in tears and covered her face with the end of her sari. But within me, nothing moved, nothing softened. I just looked away.

After a while, wiping her tears, Mrinalini got up from the sofa and said, 'True, I have no rights left. It is my suffering that I will have to pay you back with.'

'I have never sought any compensation, Mrinalini.'

'I know.'

We kept silent for long, and then I thrust a straight question at her.

'Tell me, what would you have done in my shoes?'

'Perhaps I would not have shut the door on the penitent deserter.'

With that she left the room.

I shut the door and slumped into the sofa, unable to stand up against the surges of anguished memory breaking over me: Mrinalini's cruel declaration that she had made up her mind to marry a colleague; my shameful pleading with her asking for just one chance; the failed attempt at suicide; my parents' panicked rush to Calcutta; Ghosh Jethu's calling me an escapist, a man who was not man enough; the thousand humiliating questions of the counsellor, relatives and friends; my mother's sinking into dark misery; the relentless pain; the recurrent dream of a severed limb staring at the mutilated torso...

Covering my face with my hands, I remained doubled up in the sofa, taking in the blows from a tyrannical memory that would drag me back into the square ring every time I sought to get up and reach for the distant bed.

The blows rained for ages, until I could see, through the gaps between my fingers, the darkness beyond the windows take on lighter shades of grey.

'Your turn now,' I said aloud, making a last-ditch effort to haul myself up from the sofa and vacate the place for Mrinalini. And my own words shocked me. In an instant I realized it was vengeance that was driving the persistence of memory. And the thought frightened me. It was as if I was being dragged about not by my will, but by strange forces that had always been living deep within my character, curled up in the unseen rhizome, forces that would haul me into destruction some day.

I lurched towards the bed, almost fell, but eventually made it unscathed to a corner of the four-poster. I would allow no thought, good, bad or ugly, to cross my mind, and decided to drown the persistent sub-vocal chatter in the newly-learnt nonsense of a song, 'Buddy, chill chill, just chill'.

The absurd recitation went on for a while, and when the strain had slackened a bit, I lay down, burying my face under a pillow and tried to get some sleep. But the crows and the sparrows, unaware of the torments of the night, would not let me. I tossed and turned and finally got up. The antique timepiece on the bedside table, its convex glass hurling back at my eyes the several lights on the ceiling, said it was 4.30, and I did not know what to do. My sight fell on the notebook and pen lying beside the clock—stationery Mrinalini had got for me during my stay at the hospital.

I opened the unused notebook, uncapped the fountain pen I had got Mrinalini to bring from my apartment, and tried to write my name on the cover, but the nib had gone dry. I jerked the pen a couple of times, and as the tiny drops of black ink fell on the white marble floor, a can of worms opened. With rising horror I realized that the dark drops were actually the sinister black spots in my character, spots that were alive and had a will of their own, spots that would soon spread to cover the entire floor, the house and eventually me. Scared that I was losing control, I forced myself into writing, hoping the effort would keep me grounded in sanity.

What the effort yielded is a hysterical piece penned at the crack of dawn while suffering the hospitality of a one-time lover, perhaps lying asleep in the next room, the kohl on her grief-struck eyes spreading gradually to blacken her face and her destiny.

~

But where shall I keep you, Mrinalini?

A few hours from now, with the sun perhaps a few inches above the jacaranda in your garden, I'll be returning home, with you at my heels. But where shall I keep you, Mrinalini?

Beyond the vermillion trail and then beyond the clusters of neem, sal, mahogany and mehul, somewhere near the magical mango tree, on which the stars descend at night, lies my heart buried, never to be retrieved again. For aeons have I lived, rebirth after rebirth, putting on new costumes and newer looks, brushing my hair in many a style, grooming my moustache in many a fashion, but I have never had my heart back. What shall I give you, Mrinalini?

Yes, I have dreamt of your forest retreat in many a waking dream. I have seen, in the liquid orb of a hesitant dewdrop, your lantern-lit bungalow, golden and tremulous, awaiting my arrival at the slender tip of a peepul leaf. I have watched, through the open blinds of the library, your flickering shadow on the lime-washed wall, rising every now and then and pausing at the corner, hoping to catch my approaching footsteps on the red murram path leading from the distant bamboo gate. I have sat patiently on your sagging charpoy, my bare feet on the cemented courtyard still warm and shimmering on a moonlit summer night, awaiting your emergence from inside the bungalow, your dark plaits woven with the lacelike blossoms of sal and your eyes the mysteries of Venus.

But now, with even the ashes of my dreams buried at the foot of the magical mango tree, on which the stars descend at night, what shall I give you, Mrinalini?

Besides, our unborn child lies still, blue in the cold embrace of death. I could not keep her warm, even with the embers of my unlived dreams. Who shall we live for, Mrinalini?

Mrinalini, I have played Snakes and Ladders for far too long. And come to realize that the snakes and the ladders are just a part of the ploy. You can't get home if the dice is unwilling. And the dice of my life is loaded. Otherwise, would you have left me for a cheat? Or would Sraboni have, on a trifle?

Mrinalini, I have tried morphing images for ages, taking bits and pieces from one and pasting them onto another. But it does not work. Imagination mimics reality—but remains imagination. Sraboni could never become Mrinalini. And you too will never my Mrinalini of old, be. Gunjan can never be Titir. Or Titir, Gunjan. And neither of the two, our unborn child, who lies still, blue and rotting in the cold embrace of the ashes that were once my dream. Why dig up the ashes, Mrinalini?

Mrinalini, what do you see in this dying bag of flesh and bones hanging somewhere between life and death? Look into my eyes, look at my smile, look at the twisted and mangled features. Everywhere you'll find the horror of madness, the stench of death. What do you wish to change? What do you want to put back, what to restore? I'm not yours and never shall be. Never can be.

Because you are no longer you.

Hush! Somewhere in a corner, with muffled sobs, sorrow weeps! Mrinalini, she is your sorrow, I know, dogging me with the devil's steps, rebirth after rebirth, staring at me with my dead child's eyes, tearing my threadbare frame to further shreds. Spare me Mrinalini! Don't look at me so. I see my ageless pain written on your face; I see my curse, my madness, my grave eating into your flesh little by little, revealing the sickly white of a skeletal grin.

Stop it, Mrinalini!

A few hours from now, with the sun perhaps a few inches above the jacaranda in your garden, I'll be returning home, with you at my heels.

But where shall I keep you, Mrinalini?

The Immersion

My announcement at the breakfast table that I would be leaving for my apartment in the next few hours elicited no protests, leaving me feeling somewhat foolish. It was as if all the sound and fury of the preceding night signified nothing. Gunjan, dressed in her school uniform and focused on keeping the wobbly yolk of her poached egg intact till the last hurried mouthful, merely suggested that my departure be held back until she had left, while Mrinalini called in Ram Singh and asked him to fill up the car on the way back from school. 'I will take a taxi,' I said, but Mrinalini said no.

I returned to stare at my cornflakes and milk, but before I had even had a spoonful, Gunjan put the last surviving item on her plate—an intact yolk surrounded by a thin rim of egg white—into her mouth, waved goodbye to me and Mrinalini and hurried for the car idling on the driveway. Instinctively, I got up and lumbered after her, and remembering that her exams were approaching, called out 'best of luck'. She rolled down the car's window, smiled at me and said that with her newly-grown RH firmly in place she had nothing to fear.

'See what you have done,' Mrinalini remonstrated, coming up from behind, as composed as ever. 'She didn't even rinse her mouth. And she's not even a year away from college.'

'Rhinos don't do that,' I said, copying her composure.

The mother smiled.

Somewhat baffled at the smoothness with which the events of the day were unfolding, I returned to my soggy cornflakes, telling myself that, come what may, I would leave the house a gentleman. Mrinalini, finishing her breakfast, said she had an appointment with her hairdresser at around ten o'clock and would be ready to accompany me to Ballygunge Phari by eleven or so.

'Why bother? There's no need,' I said, but was unable to find any convincing counter to her argument that she needed to show me what had been kept where after she had rearranged things in my apartment.

'You rearranged my flat! But why?' I asked alarmed, the old feeling of being intruded upon rearing its head once again.

Mrinalini's answer that I would soon find out did nothing to help.

We left Shyambazar at noon, my heart a mixture of regret and misgivings. The thought that I had perhaps bit the hand that fed me for several weeks kept turning up, getting the better of my defence that cohabiting with a single woman, that too someone who I had once sought to marry, was clearly inappropriate. Besides, I was full of foreboding. It seemed as if the tortures of the previous night would come calling any moment and the present lull presaged great storms ahead. The car moved swiftly through the thin midday traffic as I sat silent beside Mrinalini, gazing steadily through the window on my left trying to read my immediate destiny in the number of mynahs that would appear, on an electric pole, on a rooftop, on the pavement, on a tree, or in the middle of the smoky blue, which stored up in its boundless concavity the imprints of all earthly drama—to be played back in cinemascope on the fabled Judgement Day.

'One for sorrow, two for joy; three for letter, four for toy; five for silver, six for gold; seven for a secret that's never been told,' Mrinalini recited, following the direction of my gaze.

'Oh you remember that!'

'And how many did you spot?' she asked.

'Mostly solo artists, but all the numbers from one to seven, and even higher... I guess the numbers beyond seven are meaningless.'

'Not really. You could look at such numbers as multiples of two, three, five or seven. And the rest, the prime numbers, as multiples of one. For instance, eleven—the prediction for one should apply to eleven.'

'But all numbers are multiples of one,' I said and my own comment hit me. 'And why not!' I reflected, 'In fact, that is how it is: "Our sincerest laughter with some pain is fraught".'

It was as if the line from Shelley held magic. The smoky blue backdrop stretching from one end to the other was in a flash replaced by an inky blue screen which now showed a silver terrace ringed by shimmering foliage, and as I looked up I found Ghosh Jethu's burning eyes staring at me from behind thick glasses, his face lit up on one side by the radiant moon and his lips quivering as he uttered the word *dukkha*.

I turned away from the window, only to find Mrinalini peering at me, a puzzled look on her face. 'You remembered something?' she asked.

'Yeah, but nothing of consequence. Were you asking something?'

'No. We were talking about mynahs... Till you brought in a skylark.'

The conversation would perhaps have meandered into numerology but my apartment complex appeared ahead as the car took the first left on Fern Road. I turned to Mrinalini saying, 'We've reached! Wish there was someone to welcome us.'

'My wish too,' Mrinalini quipped, a wry smile on her lips.

Again, the wheel of time stuttered to a halt, the final jerk kicking up from the rut of memory a decades-old picture, almost crushed by its vintage but its colours still striking: my glowing mother, at the doorstep of our Ranchi home, beaming in her silver-and-white Benarasi, the auspicious lamp in one hand and a vermillion-and-turmeric marked conch shell in the other, welcoming Sraboni, the shy bride, and a dazed me into our decked-up abode amidst piercing ululations and Vedic chants.

'What happened, did you hurt yourself?' Mrinalini was asking, concerned, from the other side of the car, as I stood frozen, one leg still inside the vehicle and the other struggling to cope with the overwhelming weight, corporal and mnemonic. The tone of urgency dragged me back into the present, and as I extricated my remaining limbs out of the depths of the vehicle, Mrinalini came around to my side and grasping my arm urged me to be careful. 'I'm fine,' I told her, but she would not let go of my arm.

'We're making a spectacle of ourselves here,' I protested, but to no effect.

Mrinalini walked me slowly towards the staircase while Ram Singh, carrying the key and my suitcase, overtook us in a flash and was soon heard advising the security guard of the housing complex to stub his beedi and put on his cap, lest he be pulled up by his approaching sahib. We had just reached the stairs when the old security guard, with bows for legs, emerged from behind the parking stilts with 'namashkar saab, namashkar madam boudi'. And before I could take him to task, continued ingratiatingly that he had known all along I would return soon and with good news, and that my homecoming with the new madam most certainly called for some baksheesh. I was shell-shocked. Mrinalini however pulled out a hundred-rupee note from her handbag and handed it to the greedy fool.

'What do you think you are doing?' I hissed, looking around to see if anyone was watching us.

'It is you who wanted someone to welcome you. I merely concurred,' Mrinalini caught my arm again, looking at me in a strange way, the kohl in her eyes bringing back in a surge the events of the previous night.

I could not bear to look at her, and as I turned away, the row of letterboxes at the bottom of the staircase caught my attention. A notice had been stuck on mine: LETTERS FOR SUDIPTO BANERJEE TO BE DELIVERED AT H/O MRINALINI MUKHERJEE… The details blurred as I turned on Mrinalini, seething.

'Why did you stick that on my letterbox?' I almost yelled.

'Behave yourself,' she shot back. 'If I did not, and some important letter or courier arrived, how on earth would you get them?'

I had no answer but bristled in anger.

I trudged up the steps slowly, my temper rising with each painful tread even as Mrinalini's vicious grip burned into my arm. I would not pause at any landing, nor would I answer Mrinalini's repeated query if my knee was hurting. Finally, breathless and simmering, I came to the door of my second-floor apartment, only to find the profanity there too: LETTERS FOR SUDIPTO BANERJEE TO BE DELIVERED AT H/O MRINALINI MUKHERJEE… I gnashed my teeth but kept quiet, my clenched fists dripping sweat.

Ram Singh, coming out of the apartment to return to the car, handed me an envelope saying it had been slipped under the door and must have arrived after he had last visited my flat. The handwriting on the large white envelope was clearly Sraboni's. I tore it open as my heart raced, pulling out a brief letter and several typed sheets of stamped paper. Still at the threshold of my apartment, I read up the note in one breath.

> *Sudipto,*
> *Never imagined you could be so shameless!*
> *How dare you redirect me to your mistress's house? Or is she your wife already?*
> *I want my clothes and jewellery back. I don't care if you have sold them to buy gifts for that bitch. And how dare she taunt me! What bloody right did you have to give her my number? Now I know, it's my leaving you were waiting for all along. But before grabbing her, don't you think you should've had the decency to obtain a formal divorce?*
> *The least you can do now is to sign on the divorce papers attached and have them sent back to me. Along with everything my parents gave me.*
> *And don't you dare come anywhere near my daughter.*
> *What a scoundrel you are!*
> *Sraboni*

My head reeling, I hobbled towards the cane chairs in the corner and stopped bewildered. The chairs were nowhere. Instead there was an expensive sofa set sitting on a carpet. Looking around, I found even the curtains missing; the ones Sraboni had made from my mother's old Benarasi sarees had been replaced by printed silk ones. The walls looked different too, painted in different shades.

I could hear my heart thumping against my chest. Yet I did not utter a word.

Holding the wall for support, I limped into my bedroom. There, our nuptial bed was missing, replaced by a monstrosity with elaborate side tables. Panicking, I lumbered into my study. Only to find my ancient secretariat table thoroughly defaced: the cracked glass top was gone and so was the green rexine cover with Titir's scribbles. My hands shaking, I opened the top drawer and taking the key out opened the one at the bottom, looking for the only true companion I've ever had—my album. It was nowhere.

'Where is my album?' I yelled.

'Lower your voice, Sudipto! Who do you think you are speaking to? I have removed the album. I was clearing the table and saw the note your Ghosh Jethu sent you along with the sunglasses. He is right. You have to learn to cut out the glare of the past and look ahead. You have to make a fresh beginning Sudipto. The album would do you more harm. It's so very true, the past is destiny, the future...'

Something within me snapped. I picked up a paperweight from the table and hurled it at her with all my might.

Mrinalini was not as lucky as my great grandmother had been. The paperweight struck her between the eyebrows, she cried out in pain, and as she fell her head hit the edge of the sofa I had been surprised with. Blood poured out, as if from an overturned pail.

Horrified, I tried shouting for help, but could not find my voice. And as the pool of blood grew larger spreading its irregular borders on the white mosaic, I collapsed awkwardly on the floor watching with glazed eyes everything around me take on strange patterns, the last turn of the manic kaleidoscope presenting a vision of a slowly drowning Mrinalini at the far end of a rippled expanse of red waters, her right hand letting go of its grasp of tangled hair to turn towards me—a soft red palm—in a gesture of benediction...

From somewhere afar a voice wafted in, a voice I had once dearly loved, a voice now in the throes of pain, halting:

'It's all over...over... This is how it should be... It had to be paid with blood... Sudipto... I haven't told you this... Bhanu died long ago...in a car crash... But it's you I've truly loved... It took so long to know... I wanted you back... You, I and Gunjan... Oh Gunjan... Forgive me Sudipto...forgive yourself... Forgive...'

The Last Post

Thoughts leap back and forth as I fill up, in permanent black, the remaining unsullied pages of my notebook. The tiny diamonds on the clip of my rushing fountain pen do their best to put up a show: throwing bright little spots here, there and everywhere on the grim stone wall opposite, and borrowing, in their naïveté, the tick-tock of the ancient pendulum clock hanging in the jailer's cabin—to produce an unrehearsed *son et lumière* of sorts. Pity, the performance must aggravate my distress. For the relentless tick-tock also brings closer, with every lock and slide of the deadbeat escapement, what I seek to lock out, escape.

But it's my own hand that guided me into this infernal cell. It's a bargain I myself made. Standing before the dark, gavel-armed dispenser of justice, and under oath, I repeatedly declared there was no alternative. I had to put out the light. Yes my lord, I am aware of the consequences, but it was no accident. It was deliberate, premeditated. It was necessary. In fact, given six hundred and sixty-six retakes I would do the same again. On each of those six hundred and sixty-six occasions: 'put out the light, and then put out the light…'

Funny, how one must purchase justice with lies.

A few hours from now, with the sun not even an inch above the jacaranda in your garden, I'll be catching the last swing of the greased noose to steal out of the labyrinth.

Will you be there, Mrinalini?

Acknowledgements

This is my first baby—literary! And for its survival, I have to thank the several angels, shepherds and wise men who chose to be associated with its nativity, ignoring the many hazards of dealing with a debutant's handiwork. The benefactors include: the editor-cum-cheerful-rejectionist Elina Majumdar, who would extol the virtues of every draft before consigning it to the recycle bin; the impossible-to-get-past Somnath Dasgupta, who swept through the manuscript, fixing bloomers and defusing landmines; the incredibly gifted Brinda Bose, who suggested a significant change in the flow of the narrative; D.N. Ghosh, the distinguished author and essayist, who critiqued the drafts of some of the 'key' chapters; Kallol Biswas, Nilanjan Hajra and Subhajyoti Ray, buddies from college days, who devoted several nights to the rough cut, handing out suggestions; my employer ICRA Limited, especially its Chairman & Group CEO, P.K. Choudhury, who once offered to publish my short stories if no one else did; Heather Adams, who first planted the idea of a novel in me; and Vineet Jaiswal, whose persistent 'push, push' from the sidelines all through my labour was encouraging indeed.